AZTEC GOLD

CHET CUNNINGHAM

G.K. Hall & Co.
Thorndike, Maine

Published in 1997 by arrangement with Chet Cunningham.

G.K. Hall Large Print Western Collection.

The text of this Large Print edition is unabridged.
Other aspects of the book may vary from the original edition.

Set in 16 pt. Plantin by Al Chase.

Printed in the United States on permanent paper.

Library of Congress Cataloging in Publication Data
Cunningham, Chet.
Aztec gold / Chet Cunningham.
p. (large print) cm.
ISBN 0-7838-8229-7 (lg. print : hc : alk. paper)
1. Large type books. I. Title.
[PS3553.U468A98 1997]
813′.54—dc21 97-15410

AZTEC GOLD

Chapter One

Jim Steel held out his arm, and the smartly dressed woman took it, then they looked up to the stars as they walked away from the St. Louis Opera House. It had been an enjoyable, civilized evening of entertainment, listening to a bevy of sopranos from New York.

The young woman beside him sighed. "You know, Jim, I can't remember when I had so lovely an evening. I haven't heard such arias in . . . well, too long a time."

Jim smiled as he looked at her. She was young, just over twenty, with her dark hair piled on her head to cool her neck. Her face was the sort a man tried not to think about when he was a hundred miles out in the desert, or holed up in a gold mine digging ore. Her eyes, green as spring clover, caught the reflection of the gas lamps that lined the street, and in the subdued light her lips were soft and naturally red, not painted like a saloon woman's were. She had a delightful mixture of childlike innocence and maturity, that was enough to drive a preacher-man to drink.

"It wasn't bad," Jim said. And it hadn't been bad, although Jim hadn't exactly thought of going to the opera house on his first night in St. Louis. However, the girl he'd met that afternoon had hinted to him how much she'd like to go, so Jim, who liked to please the ladies, had taken her.

"Wasn't bad?" the girl said, and looked up at him. Jim felt her studying the features of his tanned, weathered face; the thick black hair that covered his ears and swept down on his forehead, his light blue eyes, and the heavy black moustache and long sideburns.

"Why, it was a beautiful performance," she said. "But I should know that a cowboy like you wouldn't appreciate fine art."

"I told you before," Jim said, chidingly, "I'm not a cowboy."

"That's what you say," the girl said, "but you look like a man who works out-of-doors. What is it that you do?"

Jim was about to answer, when he glanced up and saw that they were standing in front of the Cutler Hotel.

"This is your hotel, isn't it?" Jim asked.

She looked up. "Why, so it is, Jim. My goodness, that walk went quickly, didn't it?" She looked up at him and smiled. "Would you . . . see me to my door?" the girl asked, then looked away from him shyly.

Jim nodded, and the woman turned and stood waiting for Jim to open the hotel door. While he escorted her through the ornate lobby of the hotel and up the stairs, Jim was aware of the looks a few of the men scattered around the lobby gave the girl. She was attractive.

Down a short hall, and the woman stopped and extracted a key from her purse. She fitted it into the lock, then stood back.

"Please open it for me," she said. "I'm no good at locks."

Jim unlocked the door and pushed it open, then waited for the girl to turn up the gas lamp that glowed dimly on the wall beside the door. As the room brightened, every muscle in Jim's body tensed. Three men stood in the room, facing him, guns aimed at his chest.

Jim's hand jumped to his holster.

"I wouldn't do that," the tallest of the men said. "What's the use? You couldn't kill more than one of us, two at the most, before you got it yourself."

Jim stayed the impulse to grab his Colt .45. The man was right. Three to one weren't the kind of odds he usually bet on. He'd play their game for a while to find out what was happening.

The tallest man, who stood between the other two, smiled as Jim's hand relaxed. He was five-foot-nine, thin, with quick, alert brown eyes, neatly trimmed brown hair, and a smooth-shaven face. Jim could tell at a glance that the man hadn't spent many nights out under the stars. He must be an Easterner, Jim thought.

"What the hell's this about?" Jim asked, as he looked at the man.

"Come in, and we'll close the door and tell you."

The tall man pulled a roll of paper from his back pocket, flattened it, and held it up to read.

"Jim Steel," he said. "Wanted: dead or alive.

Five thousand dollar reward." He turned the poster around and showed it to Jim.

Jim looked hard at the picture. It was him, at least it had a resemblance to him. And the name was spelled right. But it wasn't real.

"Hell," he said, looking at the man who held the poster. "It's a fake. Anybody can have a poster printed up. I'm not wanted for anything." As he talked Jim thought quickly over the last few months, then decided that he wasn't in trouble with the law. He'd always been too careful for that.

"Maybe," the tall man said. "But for five thousand, we'll take you in and let the sheriff decide. Now doesn't that sound like too good an opportunity to pass up?"

Jim looked at the men. The gunman on the right was nervous. His left cheek twitched as he stood, his gun still aimed at Jim's chest.

Finally the smaller man, looked up at the taller one.

"I don't know about this," he said. "I mean, if he's not wanted, we could get ourselves in trouble. I don't want no trouble with the law."

"Wilson, I told you before," the taller man said with quiet force. "We can let the sheriff decide that when he sees Jim. As long as we don't . . ."

"No," Wilson said. He dropped his aim on Jim and moved back from the taller man, staring at him. "I still say we . . ."

In that instant, before Jim could take advantage of the moment, the tall man aimed at Wilson.

"Shut up, Wilson," he said.

"But —"

The man's finger squeezed the trigger, Wilson doubled over, slammed back against the wall, and then slumped to the floor, his hands on his chest. He lay still.

The tall man looked at the body, frowned, and then turned to Jim.

"Well," he said. "Now we've got something else on you. Murder. You killed Wilson while we were trying to capture you."

Jim felt his anger rise. "You don't think they'll believe that," he said.

"It's our word against yours," the man pointed out. "Are you going to come easy, or do we have to deliver two bodies to the sheriff?"

Jim had had as much as he could take. He reached for the handle of his .45 that sat ready in his holster.

Just as his hand contacted the wood, however, another, softer hand closed over his.

"Don't, Jim," a voice said.

He swung around. He had forgotten all about the girl, who stood behind him. Her eyes held his, and then she broke out into a smile.

"Sit down, Mr. Steel," the tall man said, and pushed a chair to him.

Jim did so and looked at the two men, who had holstered their guns and now stood eyeing him. The girl moved next to the tall man and looked at Jim, too.

Then, out of the corner of his eye, Jim saw the

man who had been shot move. Wilson lay three feet from him on the floor. Wasn't he dead? Jim touched the point of his boot to the man's foot. He felt a resistance. A dead man's foot would have given way to the pressure.

He leaned down and jabbed the man's torso with his fingers. The silence of the room was broken when the "dead" man burst out laughing and sat up.

Jim stared at the tall man.

"I don't know what's happening," he said. "That poster's fake, and you must have used a blank to shoot that man. I want to know what's going on here. Now!" Jim was angry, mad as hell that he had been tricked into this situation.

The tall man moved a few steps forward and held out his hand. "I'm Wilbur Judson," he said. "I'm a member of a group of men called the Secret Service. Our job is guarding President Grant. Right now, I'm on loan for another mission."

Jim noticed the word "mission." Now they were getting somewhere.

Judson turned to the girl. "You did a good job, Katie," he said, and then motioned to the door.

Katie moved up to Jim, bent down, and kissed his cheek. "It would have been fun," she said, "but a job's a job." She left without turning back.

As the door closed, Judson pulled another item from his pocket and handed it to Jim. It was a letter. Jim unfolded the paper and looked at the letterhead. It was official stationery from the office of the president of the United States, and bore U.S. Grant's signature. Jim read the letter intently, hoping it would clear up what had become a damned confusing night for him.

The message was clear and short. The president wanted Jim to accept a position to head security on a special touring display. That was all. No details, nothing.

"What's this tour?" Jim asked.

"It's a goodwill tour coming up from Mexico, a collection of dozens of statues and artifacts from the Aztecan period of Mexican history. The Cultural Commission of Mexico set it up. The display will tour by rail to five U.S. cities; St. Louis, Denver, Sacramento, Omaha and finally, Washington, D.C."

"But why should I be interested? And why would the president ask me to head up the security?"

Judson grinned. "First off, it's all gold. Solid gold."

Jim felt that old firelight up inside him. Gold. The unpredictable, dangerous gold fever ran through him as he realized that Judson was still talking to him.

"The president of Mexico specifically requested that you head the security force of this tour, and that's why our president is asking you. I hope you'll accept the job, for it would cause a serious diplomatic problem should you refuse. The president would be humiliated, if he couldn't get one of his countrymen to do a favor for the president of Mexico," Judson said, then fell silent.

Jim thought for a moment. "How much gold will here be on this tour?"

"I should have expected that question from you. You're the one they call the gold man, right?" Judson said. "The collection is valued at five million dollars, as art treasures. Even if you melted it down, it would be worth about the same in this country." Judson hurried on. "You'll be paid one thousand dollars to guard the treasure."

Jim Steel touched the crown of his hat as he stood. Yes, he thought. He'd like to get near that much gold.

"There's a tour director for the collection," Judson said. "She's a woman from Mexico City, who also happens to be the niece of the Mexican president. Her name is Margarita Josephina Maria Contreras. She's an artist who works with oils and pottery, if I remember right." Judson frowned, and then went on. "There'll be a man along with the tour, too; the director of the Mexico City Museum of Culture, Rafael Romero. I don't know much about him."

It would be an easy thousand dollars, Jim thought. He'd like to see what five million in Aztec gold looked like. He'd like to see it up close, travel around the country with it, show it off to all the pour souls who'd never see that much gold in one place again. Yes, if there was one man in the country who could take care of that gold, Jim thought, he was the man.

"I'll do it," Jim said, knowing that he

shouldn't, but unable to shake off the gold fever.

Judson smiled. "Fine, I was hoping we wouldn't have to persuade you."

"That's something I want to ask about," Jim said. "Why all the guns and the girl and everything?"

Judson laughed. "You mean our little trap? Just a way to get your attention. From what we've heard, Jim Steel is not an easy man to approach. We thought the surprise attack would work out best, and while we had the advantage, we'd explain the proposition. That way, we could be reasonably sure that you'd be listening."

Jim shrugged. "When do I start?"

"In the morning," Judson said. "Señorita Contreras will be arriving by train from Mexico City then. I suggest you get a good night's rest."

Jim walked to the door. "This woman," he said, looking at Judson. "About fifty, a hundred and seventy pounds, and ugly as sin?"

The man held up his hands. "Probably," he said. "But I'm sure you'll get along fine."

Jim walked out of the room, down the stairs, and through the lobby. Once outside, he headed for his own hotel, which wasn't far from the Cutler. As he walked, Jim could have kicked himself. How had he let the man talk him into taking the job? He was planning to rest in St. Louis for a few days before heading back by train to Denver.

Then he thought about the gold. Jim never failed to listen when that subject came up. And usually, if someone offered him a job connected with gold, he'd take it.

Jim walked briskly back to his hotel. Once inside his room, he tried not to think about the woman he'd have to be working with. Work and women rarely mixed well, especially older, ugly ones who were the relatives of presidents.

The next morning, Jim pulled his new hat down to shield his eyes from the morning sun. He had bought it the day before, after deciding that his old grey, low-crowned hat with a curled brim on each side had seen better days. Fortunately, he had found one that matched it exactly, so he felt easy in it, even though he normally didn't like new hats.

Jim stood at the train station, realizing that he hadn't asked when the woman would be arriving. He assumed that Margarita Contreras would come into town on a morning train, but no one had given him a definite time.

The niece of the Mexican president, Jim thought. He'd have to handle her carefully, so that he didn't turn a goodwill exhibition into an international feud. No matter how ugly she was, he'd get along with her. And he'd try hard to do his work. President Grant was counting on him for that.

Jim was ready to leave when a striking young woman, who was dressed almost entirely in black, caught his eye. She was standing in front of a hotel that sat across the street from the train station. Beside her was an older female, dressed similarly in black.

They looked Latin, Jim decided, and as he looked at them, they seemed to notice him. They began moving toward him as Jim studied the pair. The young woman's face, as she approached Jim, was set, a little angry, but her beauty was unmistakable; she had deep brown eyes and rich black hair, clear skin and full, red lips. Even her plain black dress, high-necked and ruffled, couldn't conceal her full figure.

The older woman was another picture. Her face was pinched through years of worry, and lined with age, browned from the sun. She looked to be sixty or older. Her hair, greying, was pulled tightly into a bun. Her eyes flickered at Jim as the two stopped five feet from him. The older one would be Margarita, he knew.

"Are you Jim Steel?" the girl said in English, with just a trace of an accent.

"Yes, ma'am, I am."

"I am Margarita Josephina Maria Contreras," she said. "And this is Tia Rosa, my aunt." Margarita motioned toward the older woman. "She is also my duenna."

Jim was surprised; he was sure that Margarita would be much older than she was, but he nodded to the women. The girl's aunt was her duenna, he thought. Jim remembered enough of the Spanish he'd learned to know that the word "duenna" meant "chaperon," and he quickly realized that he'd have to put up with two females on a cross-country tour. He'd have to work with them!

Margarita stared at him coldly, without a trace of graciousness. For a moment, Jim wondered what he had done wrong. Had his surprise shown?

"Is something bothering you, miss?" Jim asked, when the woman's gaze had become too much for him. He'd never had a woman look at him that way before.

Margarita's eyes locked with his. "Yes," she said. "There is something very much wrong. Frankly, Mr. Steel, I was expecting an older, more experienced man. You are quite a surprise."

So that was it. Well, it had been a surprising morning for him, too. "Apparently, your uncle has more faith in me than you do."

Margarita's cheeks flushed red, the first sign of genuine emotion she had shown him. She looked at him for a moment, then shook her head.

"It can't be helped now. I hope you are as good as they say you are. Nothing must happen to the collection. From the moment it arrives on our ship in St. Louis, until it is bound for Veracruz again, its safety is your total responsibility. I only pray that you take your job seriously, and that you keep the artifacts secure."

Jim had had enough of the woman's snide attitude. "I can do my job," he said. "But can you do yours? And what is it exactly that you do?"

Margarita smiled faintly. "Everything else," she said, and turned to her duenna.

"Tia Rosa," she began, and then stopped. After a quick glance at Jim, she began speaking rapidly in Spanish.

Jim grinned. Margarita must not know that he spoke the language. Jim had picked up enough Spanish in his years that he could get the general idea of what Margarita said. She was telling her chaperone that they would have to keep an eye on Jim; she didn't trust him.

"Señorita," Jim said. "If you don't trust me, why don't you get another security man?"

The young woman swung around to look at him, her lips parted. Surprise flooded over her face. After a moment, she regained her composure.

"So you speak Spanish, Mr. Steel?"

"Yes," Jim said. "But call me Jim."

"I understand, *Mr. Steel,*" Margarita said. "I shall no longer take anything about you for granted."

Jim smiled. It might be an interesting trip, after all. "Just one more thing," he said, as the young woman began to walk away from him.

"Yes?"

"Is she going along on the tour as well?" Jim pointed to the sour-faced woman, who laid a hand protectively on Margarita's shoulder.

The girl smiled. "But of course, Mr. Steel. I never go anywhere without Tia Rosa."

Jim sighed. It was going to be a long tour.

Chapter Two

Margarita smiled, looking at Jim as they stood near the train station.

"Mr. Steel," she said. "Would you care to view the exhibition's touring car?"

"You mean it's here in St. Louis now?" Jim forgot his personal feelings about the girl and concentrated on his work. He realized that he'd be doing a hell of a lot of that in the next few weeks — he'd have to, to get the job done.

"Yes, though the artifacts have not yet arrived. They're due any day now. Workmen are converting a passenger-train car in a local warehouse. It's not far," she said, and turned to her duenna. Tia Rosa gave Jim a cautious look, then turned her back on him.

Jim followed the women. Work, he told himself. Think about work. Then he'd get along fine with the women.

Tia Rosa whispered something in Margarita's ear. The girl stopped and turned to look at Jim.

"Tia Rosa has informed me of a pressing matter back at my hotel. Therefore, I shall not be able to accompany you to the warehouse. Simply tell them who you are, and you will have no trouble," she said.

"Where is it?" Jim said, glad to be rid of the girl.

"Directly behind Meyer's Hardware," she said.

"The rail tracks run right through the warehouse."

Jim tipped his hat shortly at the two women and started off for the warehouse. He knew where Meyer's Hardware was, and struck out for it at a fast pace, his boots kicking up small clouds of dust in the street.

He'd only met Margarita a few minutes ago, but Jim could tell that she was a young woman used to getting her own way. He'd have to keep their relationship strictly business; never think of her as a woman, he told himself. It would be hard. Jim admitted that to himself. He was sure that somewhere, hidden under that cold, bitter facade, was a beautiful young woman.

He walked by Meyer's Hardware, then turned down the alley beside it. Jim started thinking of what he'd have to do. Hire some security guards; that was first on the list. He'd want the car protected the moment the gold arrived from Mexico. That meant weeding through the applicants and finding the ones who were honest and reliable. It wasn't the sort of thing a man could be sure about, but Jim knew he'd have to take the risk.

He went up to the warehouse. The wooden door stood open, so Jim went in and blinked, letting his eyes grow accustomed to the darker interior of the building.

He heard the clatter of hammers and the biting edge of a saw. A half-dozen men clambered over a standard-sized railroad passenger car. As Jim moved up to it, Judson turned, saw him, and walked up to Jim.

"Glad you could make it," Judson said. "Well, what do you think?" he said, looking back to the car.

Jim studied the workman who was busy sanding off the "Central Pacific" sign on the car's side and would, he assumed, be painting in its place a glowing description of the exhibition's treasures.

"It'll look a sight better with five million in Aztec gold inside," Jim said.

Judson laughed and slapped Jim's shoulders. "That's what I admire about you," Judson said. "You know what you like, and you don't give a damn who the hell finds out." The man shook his head for a moment, and motioned for Jim to follow him as he walked to the car.

"We're going to have fancy lettering all over the outside, advertising the exhibition," he said. Judson stepped into the car, and Jim followed. Workmen were tearing out the seats and fixtures. "A walkway will extend down the left side, while the right will contain the artifacts. We think we'll be able to get a thousand people through here a day . . . probably more. That depends on how smoothly security runs," Judson said, with a smile at Jim.

Jim grunted, thinking about his security system. He'd have a guard stationed at each entrance, two or three on the grounds outside the car, and at least one inside. That was a hell of a lot of men.

"Of course, the display area will be glassed in. Nothing too good for the people of Mexico," Judson said.

"Before that, I'll be starting security around the building," Jim said. "Before the gold comes."

Judson looked at Jim in surprise. "When there's no gold here? Why?"

"Well, for one thing, I want my men to get the feel of this operation. And besides, I have to hire them soon anyway, to get them fired up for the tour. They might as well go to work immediately."

Judson nodded. "That makes sense. How many men you planning to hire?"

"Any limits?" Jim asked. "I mean, in the transportation and money areas? They'll have to come along with us, of course," Jim added.

"Of course," Judson said. "But I think if you keep the number relatively low, you'll have no problems."

"I'm thinking of about a dozen," Jim said. "That's for twenty-four-hour security. Someone's got to be watching the gold while the rest of us sleep."

Judson sighed. "I don't think I'll be sleeping until the gold is back in Mexico. It'll be worse sitting at a desk in Washington. At least you'll be close to it, when I'll be halfway across the country from it."

"Don't worry," Jim said. "Remember, you've got the gold man guarding the stuff. I don't want to see any of it ride away in the night."

"Alright," Judson said. "By the way, did you meet Señorita Contreras this morning?"

Jim frowned. "Yes," he said, trying not to think too much about the girl he'd talked to.

"And was she the ugly hag that you thought she might be?"

Jim paused. "No," he said at length. "Worse. She's young, and I'd assume, could be pretty, if she wasn't such a . . ." Jim held the comment when he saw the look on Judson's face.

"Remember, Jim," Judson said, holding back a smile. "She's the niece of the president of Mexico. You've got to be pleasant to the girl, no matter how you might feel about her. I haven't met Señorita Contreras yet; I thought she'd be arriving here with you."

"She planned to," Jim said, "but she had other things to do. I don't know what, though." Jim frowned. "I can't help it; I've got a bad feeling about that girl."

"That'll have to change," Judson said. "We can't let anything interfere with the smooth operation of this tour and exhibition, and the last thing we need is for our head of security and the tour director to fight."

Jim nodded, taking the man's warning to be friendly advice. Jim didn't take too kindly to orders, not after his two years in the army, when he had to jump when senior officers called. Yes, Jim thought, he could take a piece of advice much easier than an order.

"Think I'll go on over and see Señorita Contreras," Judson said. "If you want, you can look over the car."

"I'll go out and hire some men to do guard duty," Jim said. "Give them some practice, guarding the warehouse here. Then when the gold actually comes in, they'll be used to standing watches." Jim thought for a moment. "How long will we be on tour? Some of the men will want to know, when I offer them the job."

"About two months, give or take a week," Judson said. "And don't worry about the pay either. Tell them they'll get forty dollars a month. That should give you lots of takers," Judson said, with a grin. "Got to go. I'll see you later."

Jim watched the man leave, then looked back to the car that the men were busy changing into an exhibition car. Hell, he thought, remembering his meeting with Margarita Contreras. They'd get along just fine. Jim would treat her like she acted — like one of the men. He walked out of the warehouse, heading back into town to hire some guards.

In little over an hour, Jim had found twelve suitable men in the three saloons he had visited, promising them rail travel and money. Jim had tested all carefully in his mind; weighing their reactions when he said the word "gold." Most of them didn't react as much to that, as they did to the forty dollars a month; it was more money than most of them saw in a month's work. He'd have to keep an eye on them for a while, until he got to know them well.

Jim walked up to his hotel room and sat on the bed. He'd have to arrange a guard schedule for the warehouse, using the twelve men he had just hired. The two Secret Service men and Judson would be leaving to head back for Washington, D.C. soon. Jim was annoyed — he could have used three good men like those on the tour. But they had a higher authority — President Grant.

Jim glanced at his pocketwatch. It was near noon. He had told the men to meet him at the warehouse just before sundown, so he still had some time to figure something out.

Thirteen men, including himself. He needed three key men to act as shift heads, with three men for eight hours. That covered the day pretty well. Of course, this was just while they were in St. Louis, or when they were stopped. On the road, it would be a totally different thing, but he didn't have to worry about that yet.

Jim decided that he'd take the night shift; as head of security, he should. But he also knew that, after the gold arrived, he would probably end up working all the shifts, catching bits of sleep when he could, until they were on the train bound for Denver. With that much gold his responsibility, Jim wasn't going to let anyone touch it.

Three days later, Jim had the men working their shifts easily and smoothly. He heard the usual complaints about working during the night, but the men had accepted it in the end. Jim walked briskly into the warehouse to watch the workmen putting the finishing touches on the touring car. It was looking sharp, with gold lettering and a bright white-and-red paint-job that made it look like it was made of ivory and gold, inlaid over a lacquered box, just like the one Jim had seen in the window of a St. Louis imported-furniture store.

As he stood admiring it, he heard someone clear his throat behind him. Jim turned and stared at the man. He was middle-aged, probably over forty; slightly chunky, and greying. He wore glasses and stood four inches shorter than Jim's five-foot-eleven.

"Are you Jim Steel?" the man said, in a thin voice.

"Yes," Jim said, wondering what the man wanted.

He was obviously a city man.

"I'm David John Barlow, State Department. I am here in an official capacity to effect policy decisions concerning any legal or diplomatic problems during the course of this tour," he said, and then looked at Jim curiously. "And you are in charge of the security, I understand."

Jim couldn't help but notice a tone of superiority in the man's voice; he tried to ignore it.

"Yes, I am," Jim said curtly.

"Well, then, we shall be working closely together, you, I and Margarita Contreras. I hope you speak Spanish, because I don't understand one word of it. Not that I have anything against that culture, you understand; I simply never had any interest in learning the language. Well, now to business."

Jim asked himself again why he had taken the job. With people like Barlow and Margarita to work with, it wasn't going to be an easy thousand dollars. But the gold, Jim thought. It would be worth suffering through those two to be with the gold.

Not that Jim had any intention of stealing it. Jim never seemed to have to steal gold; it just came his way, if he gave it half a chance.

"I shall have to meet Miss Contreras at once," Barlow was saying. "There is much to discuss in regard to the tour. Is she . . . I mean, does she speak English? As I said, I don't speak Spanish."

"Yes, Margarita knows English," Jim said. "And I speak Spanish, in case you need a translation, or you can't understand something." Jim kept his voice friendly, but couldn't kill off a tense feeling toward the man. He was a pompous Washington politician who, for all Jim knew, had bought his way into the State Department.

"Very well," Barlow said. "I'll leave you to your work. If you tell me which hotel Miss Contreras is staying in, I shall speak with her."

Jim told him, glad to be rid of the man that had put another small dark cloud over the operation. He didn't watch the man leave, but studied the painter who was touching up the lettering on the side of the car.

As he stood there, one of the guards came up to him. "Mr. Steel," the small man said, scratching the three-day-old stubble on his chin. "I was just wonderin' if you knew when the gold would be comin' in here." The man looked at Jim, and then hurried on. "All the boys're a-wonderin' when, you know," he said.

Jim smiled at the man. Of course they were, he thought. So was he. He searched in his mind for the man's name, and came up with it, seconds before he started to talk to him.

"I don't know, Harris. We'll have to wait and see. It should be here any day now. That's when the real work'll start, when we have to transport the gold from the ship to the warehouse, and then guard it. So just rest easy until it comes. You'll be working harder soon enough."

Harris nodded and moved away.

That was something that he needed to talk with Judson about. Jim turned, left the warehouse, then went up to the man's hotel room. Judson didn't answer his knock, so Jim went back out to the street. A moment later, Judson ran up to him.

"It's here," he said to Jim, his face suffused with relief and excitement. "They ran into a little trouble with a storm, but everything's safe and sound. The ship just tied up about ten minutes ago. I've been looking for you."

"Great," Jim said. "Let's go see the gold."

The two men walked to the docks, Jim keeping

his mind firmly on his work. He was going to see what he would be guarding, not a prize to be had.

Jim and Judson walked down to the dock. In the broad expanse of the Mississippi a fine sailing ship, the sheets tightly tied up to the masts, rolled gently beside the pilings. Señorita Contreras stood by the dock, and allowed a man to help her walk up the gangplank to the ship. When he saw the woman, Jim stopped; of course she would be here, he thought. She was not only the tour director, but probably one of the few people in St. Louis who spoke Spanish.

As Jim stood there, looking at the scene, he sensed that something wasn't right. He motioned for Judson to stop walking and the man did so, but looked at Jim curiously.

"What's wrong, Jim?" Judson asked.

He shook his head. He didn't know, but something felt wrong. His gaze spun around to a small building that sat on the dock near the ship. At that moment, the door slowly opened and the barrel of a pistol pushed out through the crack. It was aiming for the ship, and Margarita now stood on the deck in the pistol's line of fire.

Jim whipped out his .45 and aimed for the building. Relying on his inner sense of aim, not having time to properly line up the shot, he fired. The slug slammed through the door inches from where the muzzle had appeared. It pushed the door farther open. The barrel jerked back.

As Jim ran to the shack, he noticed that several

men on the ship had turned to see where the shot had come from, and he also saw the worried expression on Margarita's face. But when she saw him, her mood changed to anger.

He ignored her and approached the shack cautiously. It was windowless, just a mass of timbers with a door on one side that lay open a few inches. Jim paused and crouched near the shack. Some of the boards had loosened and were warped. Jim pulled at the nearest one to him. If he could move it just a bit further, he'd have a clear view of the inside of the building.

Jim gently pulled it to the left. The board creaked a little. A second later, a slug flew out from the shack two inches from his cheek. Jim felt the heat of the bullet as it passed him. He lay flat, thinking out his next move. He was tempted to storm in there and shoot the man, then ask questions. But he'd like to know why the man was ready to shoot at the ship.

The man gave him no choice.

A moment later, another load of powder blasted inside the shack, and Jim automatically ducked. But the bullet had shot off in another direction. He scrambled to the side and looked at the Mexican ship. A man in a white uniform held his arm. Bright red spread out on the cloth, and his face was twisted with pain. Beside him, Margarita was still, in shock. Her face was white, and her hand covered her mouth.

"Get down!" Jim yelled at her. She turned to look at him, then realized the danger. She bent and made her way out of sight.

Jim turned and fired three times into the shack, spun around the wall, and charged inside, firing once more as he went, saving his last round for the murderous rat hiding in the shed.

But as the powder's smoke faded away, and his eyes grew accustomed to the light, he saw that there was no one in the shack. Piles of fishing nets lay in one corner, and crates and an old oar and a small skiff. The place smelled strongly of fish, but it was empty, no man, no gun — nothing. The attacker had gotten out, somehow.

Jim searched the piles of netting. No, the man wasn't hiding under them, nor was he under anything else. He simply wasn't there.

Jim cursed, then kicked at a crate. It slid across the floor, revealing a small hole in the wall of the shack. Jim squatted and looked at it. The boards had been taken away to make a hole big enough for a man to crawl through. The gunman had probably slipped through it on the far side while Jim was coming in, and then pulled the crate to cover up the hole. Simple, he thought.

Jim ran out onto the dock again. He didn't see anyone running away; the man had probably mingled in with the crowd that had gathered on the dock. The plump women and men in suits and ties milled around, talking excitedly. The two shots had attracted considerable attention.

Jim pushed through the crowd and ran up the gangplank, then stood on the ship, feeling the gentle rocking of the water.

"Margarita!" he yelled. "It's me, Jim. I've got to talk to you."

He waited, and a minute later, she appeared from the cabin, blood showing on her hand. Jim knew that she had been tending the wounded man.

"Is he hurt badly?" Jim asked. He saw the anger in the girl's dark eyes, and he wished he hadn't asked the question.

"Bad enough," she said, "since he should not have been hurt at all. You were supposed to take care of that."

"Guarding the sailors isn't my problem. The man might have had a personal grudge against the captain. It might not involve us at all. But who else knew the artifacts were coming on this ship?"

"You should have been here to protect the artifacts," she said. "That's your job."

"Then how come you didn't tell me when the ship was going to dock? That's your job, Señorita Contreras. You get your job done, and it will be a hell of a lot easier to do mine."

Margarita's cheeks flushed with anger. "There is no need to swear, Mr. Steel. As of now, I am telling you that this is the ship with the artifacts on board. I'll expect a twenty-four-hour guard on the ship until the objects are removed. Remember, that's what you're getting paid for." She turned and walked off the ship to an anxious Tia Rosa, who stood on the dock.

Jim smiled; she hadn't expected him to strike

back at her. Now she knew what she was up against.

Jim thought about the shot that had wounded the ship's captain. He immediately called out his men and placed guards on the ship, then began the arduous task of unloading the gold and transporting it to the railroad car. Since the dock wasn't equipped with railroad tracks, Jim and his men had to load each piece onto a wagon, which, when filled, was swiftly run to the warehouse, with two men riding shotgun. The artifacts were unloaded into a special locked room in the warehouse, and the wagon then returned to the dock for another load.

The gold artifacts, most of which were carefully wrapped, were of every imaginable form and size; from tiny pieces of jewelry to huge solid statues; bats and strange winged creatures and haunting faces stared out at the men from the folds of cloth as they filled the wagon.

Jim knew that every hour was a great temptation to some of the men who worked for him; no matter how honest a man was, the chance to get a piece of Aztec gold could break down even the stubbornest conscience.

Jim expected to see one of the gold statues glinting in the sunlight (or moonlight, since they moved the gold at night, as well), as a man gave into temptation. Fortunately, there had been no incidents after the shooting on the dock. Jim often wondered about that, but he had no idea who the man had been, or what he was doing.

He didn't know what one man hoped to achieve; he couldn't take over the whole ship by himself. Neither could he transport all the gold alone. The more Jim thought about it, the less sense it made. But that was in the past; he had other things to worry about now.

While the men were busy unloading the gold from the ship to the wagon, Jim took a break, relaxing in the shade of the wagon. He hadn't gotten any sleep to speak of, since the gold had arrived twenty-four hours ago and was getting tired.

Jim wiped the sweat from his forehead as he relaxed against the wood wheel, resting his head against two smooth spokes. It was comfortable, after a fashion, and Jim felt better than he had for a long time. But he couldn't go to sleep, just rest.

As he closed his eyes, Jim sighed. Just a few minutes, he told himself, just to rest his eyes.

Frank Harris sat on the wagon, his shotgun sitting across his knees. The wagon was nearly loaded; it wouldn't be long before they made another heart-stopping run to the warehouse through the streets of St. Louis. He glanced forward and saw the horses dancing gently in their harnesses, eager to get out of the hot sun.

One of the men walked down the gangplank holding a large bundle. He moved on up to the wagon, and then nearly dropped the object, which must have been one of the big figurine statues.

Harris stood. "Franklin," he said, yelling at the man. "You just watch yourself," he said. "You bust somethin' up and you'll have to answer to Margarita, and Jim Steel, not to mention the presidents of Mexico and the United States."

"Alright, alright," Franklin said, with an effort. "This thing's heavy. It must weigh more'n anything we've taken out so far. Think you could give me a hand? It'll just take a second."

Harris scouted the area. No one was around, so it probably wouldn't be too dangerous to leave his post for a minute. He noticed that Jim Steel was getting a little shuteye, and the other guard stood at the back of the wagon, his attention elsewhere. This was boring work, Harris thought; his knees were stiffening up from standing too long. It would be a good change.

Harris set his rifle down in the wagon, then jumped out of it, and went to Franklin, who stood, his knees buckling, holding the large bundle.

"It don't look too big," Harris said, walking closer to Franklin. "But gold's heavy, of course."

As Harris reached out to give the man a hand, Franklin savagely drove his boot into Harris' stomach.

"What the —"

Franklin slammed a fist into the man's chin and Harris went down. Franklin returned the other hand to the statue, so that he held it firmly, and ran.

"Hey!"

Franklin heard a yell from the wagon. The other guard had turned and seen him. Franklin saw the man lift his shotgun. After that, Franklin didn't see anything else. He was too busy running.

Chapter Three

Jim scrambled to his feet. The man's voice had pierced his sleep; something was wrong. Jim didn't worry about the fact that he dozed off; he'd think about that later.

The horses were stamping, as he saw the guard fire a blast of shot at a figure running in the distance.

Jim grabbed his .45 and sprinted toward the man, hoping the guard would stop shooting. He did. As Jim raced down the broad street beside the docks, he saw that the man was carrying something. It was wrapped in burlap, just like the statues and other gold pieces were.

He heard the shotgunner's feet pounding the dirt behind him. The thief rounded a corner and was lost to Jim's sight. Jim made the corner and saw the man, looking back, running for the sunlight at the other end. Jim fired, hoping to slow him down, but missed. The man didn't lose a stride.

A piece of cloth fell from the artifact that the man held, and then another. As the thief broke into the full sunlight at the other end of the alley, Jim saw the gleam of gold. He knew that a statue that size must weigh forty pounds. How much longer could the man hold out?

As he ran out of the alley, Jim saw that the man had slowed considerably; he was nearly walking. Jim was close enough to hear the thief's labored breathing.

"Stop!" Jim yelled, standing still. As the man turned, he saw that it was Franklin, one of his guards that he had been suspicious of, but had hired anyway.

Franklin was terrified. He dropped the statue, then broke into a run.

Jim fired, sending a bullet smashing through Franklin's right arm. He screamed as the slug ploughed through his flesh. Jim fired again. The man spun and fell, blood spreading out on his thigh. Agonized moans came from Franklin as he fell to the dirt. Jim cautiously moved up, grabbed the statue, and then approached the man.

"Your gun," Jim said, holding the statue in one hand. "Throw it over here."

"Like hell," Franklin said, his face knotted with pain. Blood spurted up out of the man's leg, and he slammed down his good hand over it, trying to stop the flow.

"Give it to me," Jim said, "and I'll get you to a doctor."

At that, Franklin hesitated, then threw his gun toward Jim. After he had tucked the thief's gun under his belt, Jim walked up to Franklin.

Before he could say his piece, berating Franklin for stealing the gold, and breaking Jim's trust in him, the guard with the shotgun and two St. Louis policemen ran up behind them.

"What's going on here?" one of the uniformed

men said. He was short, with a thick, reddish beard and dark, deep-set eyes.

"This man just tried to steal this gold statue from the Mexican government collection," Jim said, showing the gold statue. "I'm Jim Steel, head of security for the tour of the Aztecan gold."

The man looked at Jim and nodded. "You know who this man is?" he said, indicating Franklin.

"Yeah," Jim said. "I know him. I hired him on to do guard duty for me. I guess the temptation got to be too much for you, didn't it, Franklin?"

"One statue wouldn't have mattered none," he said, through his clenched teeth. "It never would've been missed."

"You better get him to a doctor," Jim said, "before he bleeds to death."

"Alright," the first policeman said. "Let's get him in a cell, and then call the doc," he said to his partner. "Is there anything broken, that you can see?" he asked, looking at the statue, and then up at Jim.

"No, not that I can notice. If I find anything, I'll let you know. But right now, I've got to get back to the rest of the gold. I'll see you later, and thanks."

The policemen nodded and walked off, helping Franklin walk. The man's groans turned into screams, as he put pressure on the leg that was gushing blood.

Jim turned to his guard.

"You did good work," he said, not remembering the man's name. "But what happened to Harris? He was on shotgun duty, too, wasn't he?"

"Yes, that's a fact," the big, gangly man said. "But Franklin must've beat him up bad, cause when I looked to find him, Harris was lyin' on the dirt holdin' his jaw. That Franklin was a tricky bastard, far as I could see."

They walked back to the wagon in silence. Jim almost expected to find the gold missing, and the men with it, but everything there was running smoothly.

Harris leaned against the wagon, rubbing his chin. There was a small cut on the flesh which oozed a bit of blood.

"You alright, Harris?" Jim asked.

"Yep, I reckon, though my jaw sure as hell wouldn't tell you that, if'n it could talk. I can tell you it'll hurt for a day or two. That damn Franklin. Don't know how he got past me."

"It doesn't matter now," Jim said. "It's over." He shoved the statue onto the wagon. "Can you make it for the rest of your shift?" Jim asked. He looked at his pocket watch. "You've got an hour more."

"Sure," Harris said. "Just shaken up a mite. That's all."

"Okay," Jim said.

Harris climbed back onto the wagon and laid his shotgun across his knees as Jim leaned against the wheels, but this time in the sun, where he could keep an eye on the men. He was going to need to keep his eyes open twenty-four hours a day, unless he could do something to ensure tighter security.

As he wiped a layer of fresh sweat from his forehead, and set his hat forward to block the sun from his eyes, Jim wondered again whether he should have taken the job in the first place. First the shooting, and Margarita's reaction to that, and now this. He'd have to try to keep this one from her.

But as he thought this, he saw the Spanish woman approaching him, with Tia Rosa, her duenna, close behind her. Margarita wore a grim, determined look as she walked through the busy port area of St. Louis, and nearly got run over by a wagon. She glared at the driver for a moment, then strode up to Jim.

Great, Jim thought. She was mad about something, but she couldn't know about the attempted theft. Could she? He had no desire to deal with Margarita Contreras at the moment, but knew that she was, in a way, his boss. About some things. He stood solidly watching her.

"Señorita," he said.

"Mr. Steel, I hope you can give me a good explanation for what just happened here." Her eyes were cold; her lips set and determined. She looked as unfeminine a woman as Jim had ever seen.

"What do you mean?" he said, as if he didn't know how she could be aware of the theft.

"You know very well what I mean," she said. "As I walked out of my hotel just now, I saw two policemen leading a man to jail. He was bleeding, and they were asking him questions concerning a gold statue that he had tried to steal. I told them who I was, and they said that a Mr. Steel had said that the man tried to rob the Mexican gold exhibit." She looked at him, satisfied that she had caught him off-guard.

Jim would have grinned, if not for the situation. He was in trouble, and the woman wasn't going to let him get around it. Still, it was laughable how the woman acted at times.

"Señorita Contreras," he said. "It is true; we had a minor incident here a few minutes ago."

"Minor?" she said, her dark eyes flashing. "You nearly let a priceless, irreplaceable piece of art slip through your fingers. What were you doing, anyway? Why didn't you stop the man from trying to take the piece in the first place? The policemen told me you finally stopped the thief two blocks from the ship."

Jim felt a twinge of anger. But instead of lashing out at her childish behavior, Jim kept his voice calm. "I was at the back of the wagon," he said.

"Not doing your job," she said.

"Margarita," he said. "I've been up more than a day without sleep. You may be superhuman, but I'm not. I need my rest. I'll admit I wasn't as alert as I might have been, when Franklin took the statue. But I got it back and everything's safe. So why don't you go back to your little hotel room and fix your hair?" he said, with forced kindness.

"Mr. Steel," she began, and then shook her head. "With this latest attempt, I must insist that you increase your security force, and that completely trustworthy men are hired. I'll have no more of these occurrences. Tell Mr. Judson that I have instructed you to hire more guards, and that adequate funding will be provided." She looked at him for a moment, and Jim thought he saw a different Margarita, a softer, more feminine girl. "And do get your sleep," she said. "We need you fit and rested to perform your duties."

Jim nodded. "Sure," he said.

"I will see you later." Tia Rosa left with her young charge quickly.

Jim watched the men transfer a few more pieces and decided that the wagon was full enough for a trip to the warehouse. Harris and the taller shotgun guard were extra alert on the way over. Jim walked behind them, with the rest of the men, a few of whom rolled and smoked cigarettes.

"Mr. Steel!" he heard a voice call in the distance.

He turned and saw David John Barlow, the man from the State Department, nearing him.

"Mr. Steel, I understand you've had a bit of trouble." The man seemed slightly amused. "I'm relieved to discover that everything came out fine. Minor problems like these are such inconveniences at times, aren't they?" he asked. "No matter. I'm sure it won't happen again. If it should, please feel free to contact me immediately, should you need my services. Naturally, I'll do everything in my power to smooth over any legal problems that might arise from the tour, or anything else," he said, and paused to take a breath.

Jim stared at the man, then nodded. "Thanks," he said. Then he thought about his sudden need for increased security. "There's something you could do right now," he said.

"Yes, Mr. Steel?" he said, surprised that his offer had been taken so quickly.

"We're going to need more men to guard the artifacts. I need some help from you."

Barlow smirked. "Surely you are in charge of security, Mr. Steel? What can I do? Why don't you hire some more locals? I'm sure there are plenty of men out there willing to earn forty dollars a month."

"Sure," Jim said. "But what kind of men are they? Men like Franklin, who tried to steal a statue today. No, thanks. I need some trustworthy men, men I can count on in trouble, that I can trust with the gold, and my life. I'd rather not worry about getting a slug in my back some night when the gold fever's running high."

"I see your point," Barlow said, tapping his lower lip. "But what can I do?"

Jim thought back to his army days. That was it, it would be perfect.

"I need twenty crack U.S. Cavalry sharpshooters assigned as guards, men who can stay on for the whole tour. Can you get them?"

Barlow seemed offended by the question. "Of course, I can get them," he said, his nostrils flaring. "I just don't know how quickly. It might take some time, some letters back and forth . . ."

Jim shook his head and broke into the man's words.

"No, it shouldn't take long. Send a message to Jefferson Barracks. That's just outside of town here. I'm sure Captain Adams can let a few of his men go, with your authorization. I need them by tomorrow morning," Jim said, with a challenging look at the Washington man.

"I'll see what I can do," Barlow said, a touch of worry clouding his voice. "I'm not making any promises, but I'll try. If only I'd been informed of this earlier. . . ."

"I didn't need them yesterday," Jim said, and grinned. "But do what you can. We need them, if we want to keep the gold safe."

"Alright," Barlow said. "I'll send a rider out at once."

"Fine." Jim caught up with the wagon and made sure it got to the warehouse in good shape, then had the men begin the unloading process. Once that was firmly started, he dashed across a few streets to the Clausen Hotel, where Margarita Contreras was staying.

But at the desk, he found that she had gone out.

"Do you know where she went?" Jim said, eyeing the desk man closely.

"No, I don't," he said. "Want to leave a message?"

"No," Jim said, and turned. Where the hell was she? He wanted to tell her he'd put in an order for twenty army sharpshooter guards.

Jim left the hotel and struck out toward the warehouse. He'd better keep an eye on the gold until those troopers showed up.

Margarita sighed and fanned herself gently as she sipped tea, looking away from Tia Rosa, who stood by her side in her hotel room. The tour had gotten off to a bad start; first, Captain Juarez's wounding on board his ship, and now the attempted theft of the statue. She didn't know whether she should risk sending the artifacts around this country, but knew it was too late to stop the tour now.

"Margarita," Tia Rosa said, speaking in English. "Something is bothering you?"

Margarita shook her head, but the old woman smiled.

"You cannot hide things from me; surely you know that by now? For twenty years, I have cared for you, lied for you, guarded you. Surely you can now tell me what is on your mind?"

Margarita put her fan down next to her tea cup on the table and looked to her aunt.

"Oh, I don't know," she said. "That Jim Steel. I wonder if he's right for the job. He's so young, and already we've had two problems with security."

Tia Rosa smiled. "Yes," she said. "He is young. But your uncle recommended him; for long, he has heard of the tales of the gold man, this Jim Steel. Is he not a better judge of men than you? Is he not older, wiser, more experienced in the world than you?" Tia Rosa softened her voice. "Only yesterday, you were a baby, and now . . . you're growing into a woman. Soon you shall marry, and have children of your own."

Margarita shook her head. "No," she said. "I do not want to be married. Not yet. I have too many other things to do. I am too busy with my work."

"The oils can wait; the brushes won't miss your company, if you settled down," the old woman said. "You've got to spend some of your life living."

Margarita shook her head furiously. "No!" She looked out the window and saw Jim Steel walk away from the hotel. She was glad that she had told the owner to tell anyone who asked for her that she had left her room. She wouldn't have wanted Jim Steel to see her this way.

Margarita herself couldn't fully explain her instantaneous dislike for Jim Steel. It wasn't that he was young; that wasn't it at all. No, there was something about his manner, his words . . .

But she would have to continue a working relationship with the man. After all, they would be in close contact with each other for the next several weeks. She couldn't afford to let the tour suffer, because of her dislike for the man. She simply wouldn't let Jim Steel bother her, she decided firmly.

Margarita picked up her fan. Jim was just walking out of sight. She leaned closer and saw that he was headed for the warehouse. Good, she thought. He should be at work.

"Margarita," Tia Rosa said.

She realized that she had been off in the world of her thoughts. Margarita looked up at the woman.

"Yes?" she said.

"Are you alright, my dear?" Concern showed on the duenna's face.

"Yes, I'm fine. I was just thinking about things, about the tour. I'm still worried about it."

Tia Rosa laid a hand on the young woman's arm. "There's nothing to worry about," she said. "I'm sure Mr. Steel can keep us quite safe."

"It's not that," she said.

"Then it's the artifacts you worry over?" Tia Rosa asked.

Margarita began to answer, then shook her head. No, it was stupid. She didn't even know what she was thinking. It must be the trip; she was still tired from the long journey from Mexico City to St. Louis. She was pleased by the city's beauty, and admired the museums and cultural events, in the short time she had been there. It wasn't much different from her native city, although it was smaller, and the people spoke English.

She sighed again and looked at Tia Rosa, who now stared at Margarita questioningly. The girl brushed off her duenna's gaze with a laugh and a wink. But as she tried to slip out of her dark mood, Margarita found herself thinking about Jim Steel again, and felt a strange quickening of her heart.

Jim helped two of his men load a particularly large gold statue onto the wagon. After packing some padding around it, to make sure the soft gold wouldn't be scratched or dented, he rested. They were nearly through transferring the gold from the ship to the warehouse. When the exterior of the train car was finished, the gold artifacts could be arranged inside the car, and the Aztec Gold Tour would open. After its showing here, it would go on to Denver.

"Okay," Jim said. "Take these to the warehouse. Then wait for the next shift of men to relieve you." It was just about time to change, Jim saw by looking at his pocket watch. He knew he needed to get some sleep tonight, and promised himself that he would — but only when the load of gold was safely in the warehouse, and his guards stationed around it. He didn't want anything to happen to the artifacts.

Jim wiped the grit off his forehead. He wondered whether Barlow would be able to get those army sharpshooters. If so, it would make his job as head of security much easier, and he would rest better, too.

The wagon was off down the road on the way to the warehouse. Jim followed it, and caught up with it as it pulled in front of the warehouse. The new shift of men was waiting there; most of them looking dog-tired, as if they'd been up drinking all morning and afternoon. The men who had been working walked away from the wagon and the warehouse, usually to the nearest saloon, before going home. The fresh men took up their positions and helped unload the gold.

As he saw to it that every man went where he should, Jim heard a soft voice behind him.

"Mr. Steel," it said.

Jim turned. "Yes, Margarita?" The woman stood in front of him, Tia Rosa several steps behind. Margarita wasn't kidding, he thought; Tia Rosa went everywhere with her.

"I wanted to know what you have done about the security problems, what measures you have taken to see that nothing like what happened earlier today will be repeated." Her eyes were cool, aloof.

"I've told Barlow, the man from the State Department, to get me twenty top U.S. Army sharpshooters from the cavalry to add to the security force."

She nodded in approval. "Can he do it?" she asked.

"I think so," Jim said. "If not, I can probably swing it. I've got a few friends here and there."

Margarita smiled. "You know, of course, that the exhibition will open soon here in St. Louis," she said. "Not many people know about it now, so the need for tight security hasn't been great. But when we let the public in, the security must be so reliable that nothing can be done to jeopardize the safety of the historical treasures of my country."

Jim nodded. "I know," he said. "That's why I thought it would be a good idea to have the army men. Not only would they be in uniform, but they're excellent shots, and I wouldn't mind if word got around just how good they are. That alone should keep away most of the trouble-makers." At least those who didn't make a living out of breaking the law, Jim thought grimly.

"Fine," Margarita said. "When will you be finished with the transfer of the artifacts from the ship to the warehouse?"

"Tonight," Jim said.

"Excellent. That means that we can begin soon. Frankly, Mr. Steel, the sooner this tour starts, the sooner we can move the precious historical relics back to my own country. I just hope you know what you are doing."

Jim nodded and looked away. Don't worry, he said in his mind to Margarita. Nothing will happen to your precious gold, as long as the gold man is around.

Chapter Four

Jim looked out the window of his room. He'd just caught a few hours of sleep, and was ready to head back to the warehouse. Twenty men in blue army uniforms stood in the street outside his hotel. He blinked, then ran out of his room, down the steps, and out onto the front porch of the hotel.

"Excuse me, sir," a young sergeant said, looking at Jim. "We're looking for a Mr. Steel. Know where we might find him?"

"Right here," Jim said. "I'm Steel. You from the Jefferson Barracks, sergeant?"

"That's right. Sergeant Foster's my name. Heard you needed some sharpshooters."

"We sure do," Jim answered. "Good enough shots to protect five million dollars in gold, for two months."

"Yes, Mr. Steel. Mr. Barlow explained everything to us. We're at your disposal. Sounds like good duty."

"I see," Jim said, impressed by the eagerness of the sergeant, and the quick work that Barlow had done. Perhaps he had underestimated Barlow, Jim thought, as he looked over the men. All were young and seemed to be in good spirits.

"Fine," Jim said. "The exhibition will be opening any day. After that, we'll be on tour. I'll arrange quarters for you while we're here in —"

"Excuse me, sir," Foster said. "But Mr. Barlow has already taken care of that."

"Then we can make up work shifts for your men, unless Mr. Barlow has covered that with you, too?"

"No, sir," the sergeant said.

Jim smiled. "Good. Let's get over to the warehouse and set them up."

"Right, sir."

As they marched to the warehouse, Jim felt better. Now Margarita would have nothing to worry about. The display would be a little safer on its long journey around the country, with the United States Army helping guard it.

Later that day, Jim and Margarita stood in the warehouse.

"Well, Margarita," Jim said. "It looks like we're all set. The gold artifacts are ready, Zeke's nearly finished painting the car, and the security force is organized and ready. When do we open the exhibit?"

The young woman looked away from him, to the train car. "Tomorrow," she said. "In the morning. We'll move the car out just before dawn. Perhaps we should put up notices . . . no, better yet, I'll talk to them at the newspaper. Yes, that should bring in some people. Everyone in St. Louis will want to see it, just so that they can say that they did. And what a marvelous way for our two countries to get to know one another." The woman smiled. "You know, Mr. Steel, even after all the worry I had about the tour, I'm excited about it now. The only reason I came along in the first place was to keep an eye on our relics. Now I can't wait for the tour to begin. I'm proud to represent my country, and help out with the exhibition."

Jim saw the conviction in the young woman's eyes; she stared behind him at the wall for a moment, before she resumed her normal manner.

"Oh! I seem to have been talking too much," she said. The girl's cheeks reddened, and Jim decided that she could be feminine, when she wanted to. There was much more to this young woman than he had guessed, he realized.

"It'll be good to open the exhibition here, and then move it on to Denver," Jim said. "I'm sure we'll have lots of people who'll want to see the display, especially in Denver and further west."

"Yes," Margarita said. "Ah, here comes Señor Romero. I wondered why he hadn't arrived yet."

Jim flinched at the name. He had heard it somewhere before, but couldn't remember who the man was. Jim watched as Romero walked up. He was forty-eight, with black hair streaked through with silver, and could be part-Indian, judging from the nose. At five-ten, with a heavy moustache and black eyes, the man looked mean. He was mad; not at anything in particular, Jim thought, but at everything and everybody.

Romero was the director of the Mexico City Museum of Culture, Jim finally remembered, as the man approached him.

"Señor Romero," Margarita said. "It is a pleasure to see you again."

The man took Margarita's hand, and kissed it while bowing stiffly. "A pleasure it is to see you, too," Romero said, in English.

Margarita turned to Jim.

"Mr. Steel, I don't believe you've met Rafael Romero yet, have you?"

"No, I haven't," Jim said, still studying the man. He extended a hand.

"Rafael Romero, Jim Steel," Margarita said.

The man quickly shook Jim's hand, then pulled his own back.

"So, you are Jim Steel," Romero said. "In charge of security on the tour, if I am not mistaken?"

"That's right."

"Do you think we will have any problems?" Romero asked. "The rail travel, the different cities we will be going to, the length of time involved? As director of the museum that owns these priceless art objects, I must be sure that they are completely safe at all times, while they are in your country."

"I'm sure my men can handle anything that might come up," Jim said. Romero was too worried about security; he sounded a lot like Margarita.

"How many men do you have?" Romero asked. "Working for your security force, I mean."

"Thirty-two, including twenty Army sharpshooters provided to us by the U.S. government.

Believe me, they'll keep your gold safe. I'm betting my life on it," Jim said.

Romero thought for a moment, then shook his head. "I'll still have to go over the arrangements myself," he said, and sighed. "When will the exhibition open here?"

"Tomorrow," Margarita said.

"That doesn't leave much time to finish things up," Romero said.

"Nearly everything that has to be done has already been completed," Margarita said, with an unmistakable air of authority that Jim saw irritated Romero.

After the man had nodded at Margarita, Jim felt that Margarita didn't like Romero. Strange. Something must have happened between them. He remembered that Judson had told him that they would be arriving together, and yet Romero must have only recently come into town. Perhaps that was why Margarita had been so cold to Romero. But then, she was usually cold to him, too. Perhaps she was always that way.

"I see," Romero said, in his perfect English. "Then I shall take another look around the touring car, to make sure that everything is alright. I would hate for the artifacts to be damaged while riding on the rails," he said.

What kind of a man was this Romero? Jim wondered. He hoped that whatever had happened between Margarita and the museum director wouldn't disrupt the tour.

Jim had to admit that he wasn't happy with

Romero's lack of trust in the security arrangements, but Jim was used to that by now, with Margarita's constant worrying. Jim decided that he would keep an eye on Rafael Romero; he seemed the kind that would warrant it.

"Mr. Steel, I have some things to discuss with Señor Romero. Perhaps you would care to join us? We're going to dine first."

"No, thanks," Jim said, tipping his hat to the woman. "I've got one or two things to do myself. But thanks for the offer." Jim knew that the woman was asking him out of courtesy, but he almost had the feeling that Margarita didn't want to be alone with Rafael Romero. Tia Rosa would be there, he realized, looking at the woman who stood against a wall, watching a boy, barely fifteen, scraping off a bit of paint from the train car where Zeke had been sloppy. Tia Rosa was protective, Jim thought, but knew when to fade into the background.

None of the tour's personnel got much sleep that night. Each was involved in his own job. Jim spent much of the night reminding his men what he expected of them, things like not using foul language, and being polite and helpful to everyone. He also had a few other words to say to them.

"The first one of you who reports for work drunk will be fired. I don't care what you do after your shift is up, but don't come to work drunk. You got that?"

A few of the men grumbled, but all nodded and agreed. Jim bore on.

"Good. Now, we've got a tough job to do. I'm sure that there's a few men out there that would give their right arms to get some of this gold. It is your duty to protect it. If one ounce leaves the train . . . well," Jim said, pausing for effect, "the presidents of the United States and Mexico won't be too happy with us."

Jim heard a few laughs among the men, and he smiled, too. But he was serious, and wanted them to know it.

"Get some sleep, those of you who aren't standing watch right now. When the exhibition's done here, we'll hook up with a train bound for Denver and you'll all be assigned seats. Just remember to lay off the whiskey and rye, and we'll do this thing right."

Jim left as the group broke up. He checked his pocket watch; almost one in the morning. Even though he'd have to help move the car out to its public viewing area just before dawn, he couldn't resist heading back to his room for a few minutes of sleep.

As Jim walked off, Zeke Slade grunted, then spat on the floor of the warehouse. Zeke was satisfied with the look of the train car, and especially with the display area inside; the rich red curtains, the shining glass panes separating the display from the viewers, the thick rugs on the floor. And the outside of the car was just as pretty, he thought: the brilliant gold and white brushwork on the glossy red background.

But he wasn't satisfied. He didn't know why, either. They were opening tomorrow, and soon after that, they'd be on the road. His hardest work on the project was over. Now all he'd have to do was watch the upkeep on the display and the car.

Zeke rubbed his eyes. It didn't matter. Everything would work out right in the end, he told himself. He was just getting stage fright. He laughed. It had been a long time since that night when the pretty leading-lady of that travelling show he was working with talked him into appearing on stage with her. He had frozen up so bad that he couldn't even move. He just stood there, staring at the audience. After that, he'd stayed strictly behind the scenes, pulling curtains and painting scenery, moving from travelling show to opera house, across the United States.

But for this exhibition, he was getting paid more than he ever had in his life. And now the work was over. Just a bit of touching up here and there would be necessary. He'd be resting easy and collecting his fifty dollars a week for the next two months.

"Zeke!" he heard a thin voice say.

The man looked down and saw the kid he had hired to help him with the finishing touches on the car.

"What is it, boy?" he said, realizing he'd forgotten the kid was still there.

"Can I go home now? My pa'll be mad that I

stayed out this late, even when I tell him where I've been."

Zeke smiled. "Sure, kid, go home. There's nothing more to do now anyway," he said, glancing at the car. It was magnificent work, and would be more beautiful, gleaming in the full sunlight tomorrow morning, when it was opened to the public.

"Thanks, Zeke," the boy said, and ran out the door.

Zeke gave the train car one last look before heading to his room. It had been a good job, he told himself. But it would get better, more fulfilling, as time went by. He'd make sure that it would, he told himself. His mind filled with plans, as he smiled and waved to the guard, and moved out into the cold night air.

"I will not put up with that man!" Margarita Contreras said, throwing her gloves across the room onto her bed. "He's the most despicable . . ."

"Margarita," Tia Rosa said. "Where is your strength, your bearing? I've never seen you act this way before."

The girl turned and saw concern in her aunt's eyes. "I'm sorry," she said. "It's just that, ever since I took over the directorship of this tour, Rafael Romero has acted as if he hated me. It is amazing how a man can change overnight. I remember at the museum social last year, how courteous he was to me, how gentlemanly. And now . . . now . . ." She shook her head and fell silent.

"It is because he is jealous of you," Tia Rosa said.

"Yes, I guess that's true."

"He must have greatly wanted to head this tour, or he would not have been affected so strongly," Tia Rosa said. "I, too, have noticed a change in the way he talks to you, the way he acts in your presence. I feel that, when you were made director of the tour, he was deeply hurt."

Margarita turned to her duenna. "I am sure he was; that is understandable. But it is not as if I did it to harm him; I just wanted to make sure that the tour was handled in the correct manner."

"Is that the real reason?" Tia Rosa gently questioned.

Margarita sat on her bed and gripped the black gloves tightly.

"No," she admitted. "Not entirely."

"And did you not want to take control of the tour because you had always wanted to see the United States? Ever since I began teaching you English five years ago?" she asked quietly.

"Partly, but I could have taken a tour of my own any time. No, I wanted to see that some of Mexico's greatest artistic and archeological treasures weren't lost or stolen. I felt that somehow the exhibition would be safer if I were along with it." She smiled. "It is silly, is it not? But that is the way I felt. Oh, Tia Rosa, I wonder whether

I should have come at all."

"Nonsense," she chided. "Of course it was good for you to come. You will see this country, from one end to the other. You will play a part in showing these people Mexico's glorious past. And you will take on new responsibilities, discover new sides of yourself. This will be an important trip for you, Margarita," Tia Rosa said.

"I hope it will." Margarita laid the gloves down on the bed and smoothed out the fingers. "So will it be for Mexico."

Tia Rosa smiled. The girl had blossomed into a fully grown woman. Now all she needed was a man.

Rosa had, at first, been against the idea of Margarita travelling to the United States, but realized that the girl was adamant and wouldn't change her mind. Although Margarita was getting too old for a duenna, Rosa had been delighted when Margarita asked her to come, knowing that there was still much that frightened and confused the girl.

As she watched Margarita walk to the mirror and let her hair down, then brush it with long, even strokes by the gas flames' light, Rosa realized that she would soon be touring this strange country. The thought thrilled her, in a secret place inside, but she would never show it. It was enough that Margarita was excited about the trip; Tia Rosa was merely there to assist, and to keep the girl out of too much trouble. That was, at times, a difficult job, for Margarita didn't mind revealing her feelings and thoughts at any given moment. It had caused some awkward moments in the past, and Rosa feared it would lead to problems with the handsome security man, Jim Steel. Fortunately, though, the man seemed to understand women — or at least Margarita — and had handled it well.

Had she seen a hint of softness in Margarita when she was near the gold man? Perhaps not, Rosa thought. But Margarita now was at the age when she was highly interested in men, and Tia Rosa hoped to steer her toward the right one.

At least, she would try!

Chapter Five

"FIVE MILLION IN GOLD! ANCIENT AZTEC TREASURES! FREE EXHIBIT!" the signs read, the early morning sunlight glinting off the beautifully painted lettering and flourishes on the sides of the train car. Women walking by with their children turned their heads to look; men on their way to work or the saloon found themselves drawn to the odd-looking railway car, that sat on a little-used siding near Meyer's hardware store.

A crowd had gathered by nine in the morning, and Jim was getting tense. His men had been acting efficiently, and no problems had come up, but he was going to be alert at all times.

Margarita, splendidly dressed in a black and white, lace-fringed dress and shawls, stood before the car, explaining in her perfect English some of the history of the artifacts that the people waiting outside would see, and also telling folks why the tour had been arranged in the first place.

Jim was impressed by the smooth way she handled the crowd; the questions, the crying babies, the lewd comments from a few of the men. Though she was still young, she handled it like a professional speaker.

Next to her stood Rafael Romero, who merely nodded his head and kept quiet. He didn't speak a word, for every time he tried, Margarita cut him off, or there would be a question from the audience directed to Margarita. Jim could tell that Romero didn't like the fact that the woman was dominating the speaking; he didn't like that at all.

Jim continually circled the car, checking for problems, keeping the crowd peaceful. He also watched his men; the ones inside the car, at each door, around the car, and the sharpshooters stationed several yards away, just in case someone got a piece of the gold and tried to run with it. Jim wasn't taking any chances.

At noon, Jim overheard part of a conversation between Romero and Margarita as the pair stood behind the car, in the shade, to rest. Jim was on his rounds and didn't mean to listen, but couldn't help it; the pair were nearly shouting.

"Why, Margarita, why?" Romero was asking. "You never let me say a word. I am able to speak too, you know. I have worked with these artifacts for twenty years!"

Margarita smiled. "True," she said. "But I am the tour director. It is proper that I should introduce the history of our artifacts to the people waiting outside."

Romero's face reddened. "No! I know much more about them than you ever will." He shook a finger in the girl's face. "You had better watch yourself," he said, his eyes to hers. "I don't care who your uncle is. I've got friends, too."

Margarita frowned, then smiled. "Alright," she said, tossing her head. "You may speak now. I should rest my voice anyway. But be careful what you say; it is important to tell the people that this exhibition is an official gesture of friendship from the Mexican government to the United States, and that we'll be travelling the length of this country, in order to —"

"I know, I know," Romero said impatiently. "I received the same information you did. In fact, I knew about the tour before you; I helped organize parts of it, remember? But then you came along. . . ." The man turned away. "Women!" he said.

At that moment, Margarita noticed Jim's presence.

"Mr. Steel," she said, as he walked slowly by.

"Yes, Margarita?"

"How are the crowds holding up out there? Any problems so far?"

"No, none that I know of. And I don't expect any, although we're ready, in case something does happen. My men are in their positions, and it would take a small army to get that gold out of there."

Margarita smiled. "You seem pretty sure of yourself," she said.

"I am."

In the meantime, Romero looked at the two, then walked back to the other side of the car. They could hear him talking to the people, and Jim decided that he wasn't doing too bad a job of it.

"Trouble with Romero?" Jim said, as soon as the man was out of sight.

Margarita sighed. "Oh, I guess not. It's just that he's been angry with me every since I took over this tour. I can understand why, but I cannot understand — or accept — his reaction. He's behaving like a child."

Jim shrugged. "I wish you two would get along better."

"It seems to me that I can't say or do anything that will get him to think better of me," Margarita said, and sighed again.

"I hope he doesn't cause any serious trouble," Jim said musingly.

Margarita looked at him quickly. "What do you mean?"

"Problems among us, the people working on the tour. That kind of thing. It can be bad."

She nodded. "I hope he doesn't cause any trouble. But every time I'm around him, I get the impression that he hates me. That man . . . something about him is not right," she said.

Jim saw the girl shiver as she said those words, even though the day's heat had already begun to build.

"We'll try to make sure that everything goes smoothly, and that everyone will get along with everyone else."

"Yes, I hope so, too," Margarita said, and turned to sit on a chair in the shade behind the train.

Jim continued his tour of the area, waving to the crack-shot soldiers he had stationed in nearby buildings, and checking with the guards inside the exhibit car to see how things were going. Satisfied that all was fine, he walked back outside and stared at the crowds.

The exhibit must be attracting nearly everyone in St. Louis, Jim thought, and pulled his hat forward. He might as well get used to this; he'd be doing it in four more cities.

In front of the crowd, Jim watched as Romero explained the history of the objects. Jim saw triumph in the man's manner, but he also saw anger, deep, boiling anger, that Jim knew would eventually explode.

The next few days went smoothly, except for the constant struggle between Margarita and Romero for attention while talking to the crowds. Jim had tried to temper the man's anger, but found it to be impossible to do; he was mad and there wasn't anything that could change that.

After nearly a week in St. Louis, Margarita decided that it was time to move on. They put notices in the newspaper the day before that said the exhibit was closing, and that they would be heading on to Denver next. On the last day, they had bigger crowds than ever. The stay in St. Louis had been successful.

At noon they closed up. Each artifact was padded, to protect it against damage should the train stop suddenly, and the doors were securely locked to prevent theft. All the windows had been boarded up from the inside during the conversion of the car, so even if they were broken, there would be no way to enter the car. It was secure and safe.

"Yes, that should do it," Jim said, as they finished all of the preparations for rail travel.

"Mr. Steel?" a voice said. It was David John Barlow.

"Yes?" Jim said.

"I've been thinking and have come to a conclusion. We cannot risk moving the car at night."

Jim turned to look at the man, who stood beside Rafael Romero.

"What?" Jim asked, incredulous.

"I'm afraid that, at night, there is a greater chance of the car being attacked while it is moving than if it were standing still. While it is still, we can station guards around it; in motion, there is very little we can do."

"True," Jim said. "But there's very little anyone else can do, either, including would-be thieves. No, we can't waste the time. We've got to keep moving to Denver."

"I'm sorry, Mr. Steel," Romero said, "but I must agree with Mr. Barlow. We should stop at dusk. I'm sure we can link up with another train in the morning. How far will we travel today?" he said, turning to the state department man.

Barlow looked over a piece of paper he held before answering.

"We should make Kansas City," Barlow said. "If we're on schedule, we'll reach the outskirts at five. The sun sets at ten after five, so that'll put us there close to dusk."

"Then in the morning, we can hook up with another train heading for Denver. I don't see why that shouldn't work, do you, Mr. Steel?" Barlow asked.

"Sure, it could work, but it's not neccessary." Jim tried to control his anger, but the men were trying to do his job. "Travelling at night on the rails is safe, but leave the car standing in the dark in the city, and you're asking for trouble. Use your common sense," Jim said. "I'm warning you. I know what I'm talking about, and I won't be responsible for anything that might come of this decision. They'll make a play for the gold."

"Who will?" Barlow shot back.

"Whoever," Jim answered.

"Never mind," Romero said. "It doesn't matter. I'm convinced that Mr. Barlow's plan is the best. We'll reach Kansas City and then stop."

"And if we don't get to Kansas City by dusk?" Jim asked.

"Then we'll stop at the first hotel and station we come to along the route. There's lots of farming towns between here and Kansas City."

Jim shook his head. "You men are asking for trouble. I'm responsible for security on this tour, but when you do things like this, you're throwing away everything I've done. I won't let you —"

"Excuse me, Mr. Steel," Margarita said from behind him. "You won't let them do what?"

"Margarita, Barlow and Romero have decided that they don't want to move the train car at night. They think it's safer to have it sitting in some city at night."

"It's just that it's impossible to guard a moving car," Barlow said. "If it's stationary, Mr. Steel can post guards around it. We can hook onto another train in the morning."

"I agree," Romero said. "It is a perfect plan."

Margarita weighed what had been said, and then came to a decision.

"We'll stop at dusk," she said.

"What?" Jim said.

"Mr. Steel, we will stop at dusk," she repeated.

Jim knew from the tone of her voice that her decision was final, but he also knew that she didn't know much about security — or about the thieves in this country.

"Fine," he said. "But I warned you." He walked to the nearest saloon and downed several beers. They were wrong, he knew. He was surprised that Margarita couldn't see that stopping the car was stupid; but then, he wasn't too sure about either Barlow's or Romero's sense of judgment. One was too emotional; the other, too intellectual.

Jim drank slowly, knowing that they would be starting the trip in less than an hour, and that he had some thinking to do before then.

Jim sat up. He had been dozing in his seat, but was now fully awake. He checked his pocket watch; five o'clock. The train was slowing down, and the sun slanted sharply in the western sky. Jim looked out his window, but couldn't see a sign of habitation in the area.

He walked up to the front of the car and found Barlow heading toward him.

"What's happening?" Jim asked.

"We're going to disconnect the car," he said. "In a little town up ahead."

"Where's Kansas City?" Jim asked.

"We did not achieve the distance previously projected for our journey," Barlow said. "However, there is a hotel with food and water, not far ahead. We might as well spend the night there."

"We are going to pull off on a siding, right?" Jim asked.

"Of course," Barlow answered, irritated. "We don't want a train to plow into the back of the exhibit car."

"That's reassuring," Jim said. "Well, gentlemen, you've got us stuck here," he said, as Romero walked up to join Barlow. "Let's see how well you enjoy spending the night in this little corner of nowhere."

He shook his head. He never should have let them do this. They were wasting valuable time, and they would be safer on the move. He hoped that they would be able to get through the night without any problems.

He walked into the car that his guards and army troops were occupying.

"We're spending the night not far up ahead. I'm sure the hotel will be able to feed us and fix us up with some places to sleep. Right after supper, I want the night shift to take up your posts around the car. Even though we're in a land where people are scarcer than pigs' petticoats, we can't let our security go slack. The rest of you can go to sleep." Jim worked out a warning signal to rouse the sleeping men, in case anything happened during the night.

Finished, he walked back into the car in which he, Barlow, Romero, Margarita, Zeke, and a few others had been riding.

"This is a mistake," Jim said again, "but we have to make the best of it." He grabbed his coat, and as soon as the train stopped, went to the hotel to get a bite of grub. It would be a long night before they were back on the rails rolling toward Denver.

The night air was cold and black. As luck would have it, the moon hung as a thin crescent in the eastern sky, emitting no light. The stars, brilliant as they shone, did little to illuminate the flat land.

Jim pulled his coat tighter around him; thinking how Margarita, Barlow, and Romero were snug in their beds in the hotel, while he had to stand there watching the car. He knew that he didn't have to, but if he wanted to ensure the gold's safety, he'd have to perform above-and-beyond.

Jim listened to the stillness. He had given strict orders that his men not talk with each other while they stood their watches; he didn't want them to be distracted, and miss something that they should have seen or heard.

Jim looked up. Something snapped in the distance, away from the car and the hotel. He then heard the soft plod of hooves on dirt. Jim grabbed his Colt .45 and searched the darkness. Nothing moved. The night was still again. Had he imagined it?

Jim walked slowly around the car, searching every part of the surrounding land. The thin moonlight gave him only vague outlines of trees and rocks, but he looked anyway, in case he caught the glint of metal or the eyes of an animal. All he could see was the hotel on one side, and on the other, a ramshackle scarecrow, that looked like it had been abandoned years ago in a field that had gone to seed.

One of the guards spoke to him, but Jim cut him off with a sharp motion of his hand. Someone or something was out there, he knew. He wondered when it would make its appearance.

Hooves, then a muffled cry from the other side of the train car. Jim raced there and found one of his guards missing. His .45 ready, Jim listened, eyes straining to pierce the darkness.

"Git that car open!" he heard a rough voice say in the distance.

Jim fired in that direction, but knew he would miss, not having a visible target to shoot for.

Jim heard more shots; some from his own men, he guessed. The darkness made the whole situation ridiculous; they couldn't see what they were firing at.

"Under the car!" he ordered, and then whistled. The guard closest to the hotel dashed to awaken the other men.

A slug whispered two feet from Jim's face and slammed into the train car. Lying under it, Jim heard the wood splinter and crack, then horses neighing all around him. They were surrounded.

A horse came into Jim's view. He shot at its rider, who fell back off the horse, and the beast stamped and ran into the darkness.

His other men, holed up under the car with him, were busy engaging unseen gunmen on either side. Jim heard a yell and saw a man fall to the ground dead from another horse. A second slug rammed into the car above them. Jim fired wildly in the direction the shot had come from.

The lights came on in the hotel and his men began pouring out, guns ready. A few fired shots to let the thieves know they meant business.

Shots volleyed in the darkness; Jim heard oaths as men took slugs. A moment later, he heard several men ride away fast, and he called his own to hold their fire.

When they did, there was silence. Jim hoisted himself up from under the car and looked around. In the eastern horizon, the sky was just beginning to be touched with dark blue; sunrise was near. Jim checked over his men. Four had been wounded, none seriously, and they had two bodies. None of his men recognized them, so they must have been attackers.

Jim next inspected the train car. It was still locked, unviolated, although the wood had been splintered in two places.

Margarita ran up, wrapped in a heavy robe.

"What happened?" she asked breathlessly.

"Just what I said would happen," Jim said. "We had a surprise visit."

"Is anything missing from the train car?" she asked, looking at the holes.

"No, they didn't get inside. They wounded four of my men, but we killed two of theirs."

Margarita looked at him. "But I do not understand," she said. "How could they have known who we were, and that we would be here?"

"Listen, lady, lots of men make gold their lives. They probably knew the Aztec gold would be coming through here before you or I did. They make it their business to know. That much gold can't be carted around here, without every outlaw and thief in the area knowing about it."

Margarita's face was glum in the growing light.

"I thought it would be safer," she said. "Here, with nothing around." She motioned to the land.

Jim shrugged and frowned. "Barlow," he said, "get over here. You, too, Romero."

The two men walked up to Jim.

"Yes?" Barlow said. "You wished to speak about something?"

"Yes," Jim said. "No more night stops. I don't care what the hell any of you think. We'll keep on moving until we get to Denver, day and night, and we won't have to go through this again," he said, pointing to the bodies and his wounded men.

"But —" Barlow began.

"No buts!" Jim said. "You've already got four of my men wounded. Another night like this, and you'll turn some into corpses. I'm in charge of security, and I'll decide what we do, or don't do, when it involves the safety of the artifacts."

The Washington man was silent, and Romero stared at the rising sun.

"Let's get some food and get back on another train, if one comes by this hellhole," he said. Jim walked to the hotel, leaving Romero, Barlow and Margarita staring after him.

He didn't care what they thought; he'd had his fill of prissy government men and hardheaded museum directors. His job was to guard the gold, and he'd do it, no matter who tried to stop him.

Chapter Six

Zeke Slade stared out the railroad car window, watching the flat, featureless land roll by. In the distance, he knew, stretched the Rocky Mountains, but for now, there wasn't much to see. And he was bored.

He looked around the railroad car. Most of the other principal members of the tour were dozing, or chatting with one another. There was Margarita Contreras, whispering to that older woman that was always with her — Tia Rosa, he had heard her called. Barlow and Romero were discussing something, too, over in a pair of seats on the right farthest from Zeke. Jim Steel, head of tour security, touched the brim of his hat and yawned.

There were a few other passengers in this car, but they weren't members of the tour, just people on their way to Denver.

Zeke thought about the attempted theft of the gold that had happened the day before, near dawn. It had been a bungled job, he thought, very unprofessional. Why, he could figure out a much smoother, easier way to get that gold . . . or at least, some gold.

First off, he wouldn't try a slam-bang assault; no, he'd have everything planned out in advance, leaving nothing to chance. He'd have to get the guards out of the way first. Once he did that —

and he'd have to do it without shots, so that the others wouldn't be alerted — he'd go for the treasure carefully, quietly.

Then Zeke smiled. It was a ridiculous idea. He had no reason to risk everything to steal the gold. Besides, he was alone. No way to do something like that by yourself. And he could loaf for the next two months, and get paid for it. Not bad for a man who'd worked his butt off for nearly thirty years.

But all that gold, Zeke thought. It was sitting there waiting to be taken. To do it, a man had to be smarter than Jim Steel. That's what it all boiled down to. Steel was the keystone that kept the whole thing together. He'd have to be smarter than the security man.

The obvious way, Zeke thought, was to go for the obvious — to catch them off guard, strike when and where they would never expect it. That would work perfectly. But again, he couldn't work alone. Not on this kind of operation. He had to have a trusted partner.

Again Zeke smiled at the idea, then shook his head. No, he wouldn't want to risk everything for a fool's chance to get that gold . . . or would he?

If he did get it, he'd be living easy for the rest of his life. Why, he could open up his own opera house and bring all the best girl singers in from New York. He'd find a quiet little town somewhere that showed promise, and bring it to life; get in on the ground floor of its development and growth. He'd be able to multiply his wealth ten times over within a few years.

All it took was a few carefully thought-out moves, a good partner, and a lot of nerve. No man would say that Zeke Slade didn't have nerve; he had the guts to go on against impossible odds. Hell, he'd do nearly anything once. But this was something different. He'd been on the wrong side of the law a few times in the past, but had never been caught. Maybe his luck would hold out for just one more job, one that would secure him a safe and rich future. If that luck would hold out just a little longer. . . .

Zeke planned quickly. They would be in Denver by tomorrow, he'd heard someone say. That didn't leave him much time, but he knew he didn't need much time. All he needed was opportunity, and a good man.

Zeke looked out the window, but this time he smiled. He had the chance of a lifetime riding right there with him on that train. Could he possibly let it slip through his fingers before he had the chance to make use of it?

"Denver," Jim said. "It's not as big as St. Louis, and it's rougher, not as civilized."

"Do you think we will have any problems there?" Margarita asked, as they sat beside each other on the train, listening to the steady sound of the wheels below them.

Jim frowned. "I can't say for sure, but I don't think so. We'll make it clear that we've got guards surrounding the exhibit. If someone does get gold fever, we'll take care of him. Don't worry," Jim said, looking at the young woman.

"I am not worried. It is simply better to go over all the possibilities that might occur, so we're prepared for them. The idea of those twenty guards from the army was a good one; they may save us yet," she said softly, rubbing her hands together.

"Are you sorry you came?" Jim asked suddenly, noticing her mood.

"No," she said at once, looking at him and smiling. "I'm just a little tired, not used to trains. It can be exhausting — like the time the train had to stop suddenly," she said.

Jim smiled, as he remembered the incident. He had had a cup of coffee and had just tipped it up to his lips, when the train braked and everything else lurched forward. Fortunately, the coffee wasn't steaming hot, so it didn't burn him badly, as it splashed onto his face and dripped down to his chest. But it had taken him by surprise. He looked around the car and saw nearly everyone in similar situations. At least one man had fallen flat on his face in the aisle between the rows of seats, while a young woman found herself lying across a man's lap. The man had graciously helped her back into her seat.

Jim laughed out loud at the picture. As he did, he noticed Margarita's quizzical stare, and then Romero, seated several rows in front of him, turned back to look at Jim.

"What on earth are you laughing about?" Margarita asked.

"The train," Jim said, his humor gone as he looked at Romero. "About the time it stopped suddenly."

"I see," Margarita said. "Now, getting back to work. We should arrive in Denver tomorrow, Tuesday, in plenty of time to open the exhibit on Wednesday. This will leave us several hours to arrange for hotels, alert the newspapers — is there more than one? — and to establish security procedures."

"You left out one thing," Jim said, surprised to be saying it. Over the past few days, Margarita had shown more of her true spirit; the young, intellectually mature, but emotionally volatile, young woman under the polish and airs. And he had, for some damnable reason, found himself liking the girl. He couldn't understand why.

"What did I leave out?" Margarita asked, looking at him with a curious expression on her face.

Jim remembered the girl's duenna, who sat one row behind them. He lowered his voice accordingly.

"Dinner? With me? Tonight? I know the best restaurant in town," he added.

Margarita looked at him for a moment, and then lightly blushed.

"We'll see," she said. "I'll be so busy arranging things tonight for the exhibit. I don't see how I can get away from them to have dinner with you."

"But you have to eat," Jim pointed out. The girl seemed interested; maybe she didn't like talking in front of her duenna, Jim thought.

"Yes, that's true," she said.

Jim pressed further.

"So it's a date?"

She looked at him and her eyes softened. "Alright," she said. "Dinner tonight."

Jim smiled. Margarita looked surprised, but pleased that he had asked her. And almost as if she was surprised that she had accepted his offer.

"Shall I dress formally?" she asked, straightening the hem of her skirt that fell around her ankles.

"Sure," Jim said. "And I'll get a little spiffied up, too. I promise you, you won't be disappointed," Jim said, and smiled.

At this, Margarita grew uncomfortable; she began fanning herself with a delicately carved wood-and-paper fan, and looked out the window.

"We shall see, Mr. Steel," she said. "We shall see."

"Call me Jim." He said it quickly, to catch her off guard. He succeeded; for a moment, the woman's manner faltered, but she brought it back under control.

"We shall see, Jim." She threw him a quick glance.

He stood. "Thanks for our talk," he said, and went back to his seat. As he walked down the aisle, Tia Rosa gave him a look, and then took her place beside Margarita. She whispered something to the girl, but Margarita continued to gaze out the window, as though deep in thought.

Jim eased himself into his seat and tried to relax for a few minutes. He wondered why he had asked Margarita out to dinner. To talk about business? Yes, he decided. That, and to show her Denver . . . while, at the same time, showing Denver Margarita Contreras.

Jim looked at Barlow and Romero, who sat in front of him. The men had quickly forgotten the pre-dawn attack on the exhibition car, which had been their own damn fault. After the wounded men had been patched up, everything returned to normal. But it stuck in Jim's mind; he'd never let Barlow and Romero order him around again. Not when the orders threatened to breach their security. He'd let them do their jobs, as long as they allowed him to do his.

As he stared at the men, Romero turned to look at Jim. Though Romero looked away quickly when his gaze met Jim's, the latter couldn't help but feel the anger in the man's eyes.

They pulled into Denver and positioned the exhibit car on a siding arranged for them near the center of town. Margarita at once went to the local newspaper, the *Rocky Mountain News*, trying to stir up some excitement about the exhibit. Naturally, word of them had spread before their arrival, and many curious faces watched as they pulled into town, the car glittering in the hot afternoon sun.

Jim went directly to the Denver House, his favorite hotel in the mining city of Denver.

"Hello, Jackson," Jim said to the elderly man at the desk.

"Why, Jim Steel, how're you?" he said, squinting against the light that came in through the door. "You be stayin' long? Want your regular room?"

The man hadn't changed. Frank Jackson had run the Denver House for as long as Jim could remember. He always stayed there when he was in Denver, and always in the same room — 321, in the corner of the building, where he had a clear view of the street below him.

"Yes," Jim said. "Still know the number?"

"Yes, yes, course I do. Three twenty-one." Jackson scratched his head as he reached for a piece of paper. "Yep, three twenty-one. How long you be plannin' to stay, Jim?"

"Don't know. Probably three, four days at least. I'm here with that gold exhibit."

"Gold exhibit?" Jackson repeated. "Oh, the Mexican one. Yes, that's the most gold that's been around here for a while. 'Cept the mint, of course," he said, and laughed.

"I'm doing security on the exhibit," Jim said. "So I'll be here as long as it is, then I'll be moving on."

"Well, it's good seeing you again, Jim," Jackson said. "Just keep out of trouble and let the women alone, and you'll live a long life." He pulled at his short white hair.

Jim smiled as he listened, for the hundredth time, to the man's advice.

"Just thought I'd stop in and tell you I'm in town. I've got some things to do first, but I'll be wanting a bath right around six. Can you fix it up?"

"Sure, sure," Jackson said. "Bath at six for Jim Steel. It'll be ready."

"Thanks."

Jim left the hotel and walked south along Ellsworth Avenue. There was one more thing he had to do, before he checked on his savings accounts in the banks of Denver. He had an old friend to visit.

The livery stable was dark, and Jim didn't see the owner around, so he walked in. After checking a few stalls, he saw a familiar face.

The buckskin was resting, his feet splayed out and leaning against the stall wall. When Jim walked up to him, the horse neighed.

"Hamlet," Jim said, stroking the horse's mane. "How've you been?"

The horse was happy to see him; Jim had been away nearly a month, and had missed the buckskin himself.

"Who's there?" a voice behind Jim said.

Jim turned. "Jim Steel," he said. "This is my horse, Hamlet."

The voice turned out be a boy's, deep for his fifteen years. He held a .44 in his right hand,

and he approached Jim cautiously.

"My pa's away right now. You say this here's your horse?"

"Course it is," Jim said. "When I left last month, I gave your father enough gold to look after Hamlet until the day of doom," he said. "So put your piece away before someone gets hurt."

Hamlet shook his head around as Jim continued to rub his neck.

The boy's shockingly red hair and freckled face were proof enough that he was Curly's son; the Irish blood showed as plain on his face as anything could. This was definitely Curly's boy.

"You plannin' on takin' him?" the boy said. "you can't. Not until my pa gets back."

"No," Jim said. "I'm riding the train right now. Just wanted to stop by and see how he's doing." Jim looked the buckskin over. "He seems to be eatin' all right. Is he getting exercised?"

"Sure," the boy said readily. "He gits rid ever' day, and brushed down. He's in real good shape."

Jim admitted that Hamlet hadn't looked nearly that good when he'd left him there. Jim had ridden him long and hard, and the horse had deserved a rest. That's why he'd taken the train to St. Louis.

"You tell your pa that, if he needs some more money, he should see me over at the Denver House. That's where I'll be stayin' for the next few days. You got that?"

"Sure," the boy said.

Jim turned back to Hamlet.

"I'll see you later, alright?" he said, patting the horse's rump. The animal-actor whinnied and nodded, as Jim remembered how he'd bought the horse from a travelling theatrical group. Hamlet had bitten the leading lady, and they were eager to get rid of the animal. He'd seen Jim through some rough spots over the years of their partnership.

"You remember to tell your father, alright?" Jim said to the boy, as he turned and went to the street.

"Sure," the boy said.

Jim walked to the Commonwealth Bank. He had some accounts that needed checking up on, just to make sure that all that gold he'd deposited hadn't run off somewhere.

"Hey, take it easy!" Jim said. "That's plenty of water." He sat in the tin tub, his knees sticking up above the level of the nearly scalding water.

Jackson shrugged and pulled the pail away. "Alright, if you're sure."

"Thanks," Jim said, then relaxed into the warm water, thinking about his date later that night with Margarita Contreras. He wanted to be as proper-looking for the woman as he could; thus, the bath. It was a bother, but it did feel good. Jim only wished it were easier; then he might take a dip into the warm water more often. He sighed and scrubbed his back, then his face and hair.

After soaping himself thoroughly, Jim took one of the pails of fresh water that Jackson had left near by and lifted it over his head. He tipped it, and the cold water spilled down on him, washing away the soap. It woke him up completely after the hot bath. His skin tingling, Jim dried off quickly, and dressed in the new pair of pants and shirt that he'd bought that afternoon. After that, he returned to his room, and after checking to see that he was still clean-shaven, left to go to Margarita's hotel.

The New Sherman Hotel was elegant for Denver's rugged, remote location. Jim walked in and admired the chandeliers and thick rugs on the floor, but he had other things on his mind. He had to make this a pleasant evening for Margarita. He checked his watch and saw that it was seven o'clock exactly.

Jim knocked on the door and waited.

"Just a moment," he heard, from behind the thick, solid oak door.

Jim tapped his toot on the floor impatiently. Women always kept a man waiting. Then the door opened.

Margarita was dressed in a tight-waisted, pure-white dress, pearl buttons running down the front, and masses of ruffles in the skirt. Jim had never seen her so beautiful.

"Good evening, Jim," she said. "I hope that I am dressed appropriately for the evening," she said.

"Yes, fine," Jim said, and coughed. "Prettiest

girl in Denver," he added.

She blushed. "I heard from Mr. Barlow that there weren't many women in Denver. Why, he said he walked around here all day one time, and saw only five women."

"That was some years ago, I'm sure," Jim said, still studying her appearance. Her hair had been delicately drawn up on top of her head, with tiny curls cascading down the back of her neck. Beautiful silver earrings completed her costume.

"It's true, though," Jim said. "There aren't as many women in Denver as there are in St. Louis. So much more will Denver appreciate you."

She looked away from him. "Thank you," Margarita said. "Well, shall we go?" She opened the door wider.

Jim put out his arm to take her. Margarita's delicate fingers closed around it gently and she walked out into the hall. As Jim reached back to close the door, however, he was surprised to find Tia Rosa, her face expressionless, move from the room to stand behind Margarita. She too was dressed for going out, though not nearly as spectacularly as Margarita.

Jim was surprised, then mad, but kept his silence. He remembered that Margarita had said that Tia Rosa went everywhere with her. He had forgotten that; when he asked Margarita to go to dinner with him, he'd assumed that they'd be alone for the date. Margarita wouldn't argue the point with him, he was sure, so he swallowed his comments and led Margarita down the hall, with her aunt following behind.

He sighed as they walked into the deepening twilight. Nothing he ever did with Margarita turned out the way he expected — or wanted — it to.

The dinner was great, as it always was at the Hanover. Jim was amused at Margarita's delicate manners and careful conversation, as if she didn't want to say anything that Jim might take personally, aware that she was under her duenna's watchful gaze. Jim sat between the two women and found it damn hard to say anything at all. During the dinner, Margarita had fallen into the habit of using his first name, something that Jim liked, and that was not lost on Tia Rosa.

Conversation, under the circumstances, was limited entirely to work; about Denver, and how it would receive the exhibit. Margarita asked a few questions to ensure that the security would be tight; Jim assured her that all was well. He had even added one man onto the night shift, just in case. He knew how this city was . . . it was still a wild mining town in many ways.

When dinner was over, Jim took Margarita back to her hotel, with Tia Rosa following them. After a few words at the door, once the older woman had gone to her own room nearby, Margarita looked up at Jim.

"Jim, I had a lovely evening," she said. "I hope we can do it again sometime."

"Yes," he said, agreeing with everything that she said.

Margarita held out her hand, and he took it. She pulled it back a moment later, as if to break the physical contact between them.

"Good night, Jim," she said, and closed the door quietly.

Jim nearly threw his hat on the floor. He hadn't kissed her. He walked back to his hotel, frustrated, then turned into the first saloon he passed. He needed something to tide him over.

Zeke Slade walked slowly, cautiously, to the exhibit car. He knew who he had to talk to, who could help him with his problem. And if he was right, the man would be working tonight, guarding the exhibit car.

"Who's that?" one of the guards said, his .45 drawn and ready.

"Hold your fire," Zeke said. "It's me, Zeke Slade."

"Oh, Zeke," the guard said. "For cryin' out loud! You scared me more'n a rattler in my boot. What the hell you doin' out here?"

"Came to talk with Rufus. He around?"

"Sure, the other side, near the rain barrel."

"I've got to talk to him."

"Well, go ahead, I ain't a-stoppin' you," the guard said. "But don't you go takin' too much time. Mr. Steel won't like it, if he catches Rufus skylarkin' around."

"Don't worry," Zeke said. "He won't." He

moved on around the car and saw Rufus standing, sure enough, next to the water barrel that caught the runoff from the roof of Polkson's Dry Goods store. He leaned against a post enjoying a hand-rolled smoke.

"Rufus," Zeke said, approaching him.

"That you, Zeke?" he said, his face gaunt and weathered beyond his years. The man was young, thin, wore his clothes badly, and had a dull, monotonous voice. His green eyes were always shifting and searching. He rhythmically inhaled on the cigarette as he watched Zeke approach him.

"Yes, it's me, Rufus," Zeke said. "I've got a job for you, Rufus, and I think you'll like it." He kept his voice low, so that the other guards, all out of sight, wouldn't hear him.

"Yeah?" Rufus said. "What kind of job?"

"A job that'll get you a little piece of heaven, if you decide to take it."

"Huh?" Rufus said.

"It's easy, and I've got a foolproof plan," Zeke said, whispering into the man's ear.

"Hey, you ain't a-talkin' about the Aztec gold, are you?"

"Don't worry," Zeke said. "It don't have nothing to do with that. It's a big payoff, anyway, big enough to make your eyes water."

"So start talkin'," Rufus said.

"When you get off work?"

"I'm on half-shift; I'm off at two."

Zeke nodded. Everything was fine so far. As he told Rufus of his plan, he grew bolder and surer of himself. Rufus wasn't a seasoned criminal, but he had the lack of scruple and intelligence that practically ensured that he'd be the ideal partner in crime.

The plan would work, Zeke knew. It had to. It was perfectly worked out — strike them where they'd never expect him to. If he could rely on Rufus he'd be okay. The man had a reputation among the tour personnel of being a strange guy. Zeke didn't care about that, as long as he could move fast and do what he was told to do.

After a few minutes Zeke went back to his hotel room. Everything depended on Rufus now. Zeke couldn't do it alone.

Margarita awoke. It was dark and cold. She saw that the window was open. The wind shot through it, picking up the curtains like flags in the breeze. The sudden wind chilled her, so she wrapped a robe around her, and walked to the window. As she looked out, she remembered that she had left the window shut; in fact she remembered trying to open it, and finding that it had no handle. Now it was open.

Fear spread through her. What should she do? The room, dark in the corners, now seemed to close in on her. Margarita turned and ran for the gaslamp next to the door. The light would help her concentrate, she told herself. Just as Margarita reached up to turn the flame, hands closed around her from the back.

Margarita's scream was cut off by greasy fingers that slammed down over her mouth. Another hand tightly gripped her waist. Margarita, frantic, tried to bite the hand. She kicked at the legs, but the man dragged her across the floor, apparently unheeding of her efforts to free herself.

Terrible thoughts rushed through her mind; she had heard what happened when strange men got into women's bedrooms at night. If only she had gotten a second-floor room, she thought, it wouldn't have been so easy for the man to have gotten in. On the ground floor, she was just asking for people to come in. But the lock, she thought. It had been broken. She couldn't open the window.

She slapped, her eyes closed in frustration and fear, at the face of the man who dragged her along, making strange noises in her throat when she tried to talk.

"Shut up," the man said.

His hand shifted slightly over her mouth. Margarita's teeth sought out, found, then sank deeply into the flesh of the man's hand. She heard him cry out, and hoped he'd pull it away, so that she could scream. Instead, he pressed it harder against her. Blood seeped from the wound she had inflicted, and smeared across her lips, and the taste and realization of what it was made her feel faint.

"Bitch," the man said, and a moment later, Margarita felt a sharp pain on her head.

She shook it, but the pain increased. The taste

of blood and the pain were too much for the delicate girl, and she blacked out.

Zeke noticed that Margarita had gone limp, and grinned. Good. Nothing was harder to carry than a kicking, mad-as-hell woman. He pushed her through the window, into Rufus's hands, then climbed out himself. They carried Margarita to a horse and draped her over the saddle. Rufus went to the window, climbed into Margarita's room, and laid a carefully lettered note on the woman's bed. He hurried back to his horse, and the two men, with the woman tied onto the one horse, rode out of Denver, confident that their scheme would soon make them rich.

Margarita, unconscious and bound, didn't see the passing scenery, nor could she be afraid of what these two men would do to her in the wilds.

Someone was knocking on his door.

"Mr. Steel! Mr. Steel!" a woman's voice said.

Jim shook his head, sat up in bed, and pulled on his boots and shirt. He walked to the door and opened it.

Tia Rosa stood in tears.

"Yes?" he asked her.

"Mr. Steel," she said, "they've taken Señorita Contreras, my Margarita," she said, wiping her eyes.

Jim strapped on his holster and ran to the New Sherman Hotel, leaving Tia Rosa to catch up with him. There, Barlow and Romero stood in Margarita's room, along with a few other men, looking at a piece of paper.

"We found this on her bed," Barlow said. "Well, actually, her guardian found it."

Jim took the piece of paper and read the first few lines. "IF YOU DON'T LEAVE 200 POUNDS GOLD AT CLEARWATER SPRING SHES DEAD."

Jim stared at the note. He hadn't expected this, hadn't been prepared for it. Margarita had been kidnapped, someone was demanding two hundred pounds of gold, and he was stuck in the middle of it.

Chapter Seven

In Margarita's room, Jim glanced at the note that had been found on her bed by Tia Rosa, just after she discovered the girl's disappearance. There were more words on it: "DONT MOVE THE EXHIBIT CAR OR ITLL BLOW UP. I PUT A BOMB IN IT YOULL NEVER FIND."

They wanted two hundred pounds of gold. That was a lot of money, more than $66,000. Jim had no idea of who had done it. No clue. And why kidnap Margarita? Why not just steal the gold?

Jim couldn't believe what had happened; it was so unexpected. A young man came into the room.

"Mr Steel?"

Jim looked at him. "What is it?" he asked the man, whom he recognized as one of his guards.

"Zeke Slade and Rufus Holmes are missing," he said. "I thought you would want to know."

"Thanks," Jim said, and the man left. Zeke Slade and Rufus Holmes. Could they be responsible? Who better to know how and where to rig a bomb in the train car than Zeke? He'd been there while they converted the car from carrying passengers to housing a travelling exhibit. He could have planted the bomb at any time, and only now activated it, so that the slightest movement would set it off. They couldn't open the exhibit now, until Zeke and Rufus were found

— and Margarita, for that matter.

"Mr. Steel," David John Barlow said. "Concerning that two hundred pounds of gold. I will contact the Denver Mint at once, and have the gold at your disposal as soon as possible, within a few hours, I should think."

"Thanks," Jim said. He'd play the kidnappers' game, as long as he was in the dark. If it was Zeke and Rufus, they'd made it pretty obvious by not trying to cover their absence. Were they that sure of themselves?

Clearwater Spring. Not far, perhaps five miles out of town. Jim remembered the spot; tall cliffs on both sides, plenty of brush and rocks. A perfect place for an ambush. Jim knew that, when he rode out there, he would have to be careful.

"Barlow," Jim said. "Don't open the exhibit today, and don't let anyone — even one of our own men — inside. We'll postpone the opening until this thing is cleared up. And forget about the gold, too. I don't need it."

"But the note," Barlow said.

"Never mind the note. I'll take care of everything. I know what they're doing."

"I don't understand," Barlow said. "Aren't you going to try to get Margarita back?"

"Of course," Jim said, irritated. "But not that way. Not their way." He turned to face everyone gathered in the room. "Everyone stay in Denver. Don't go out to Clearwater Spring, 'cause you're liable to get shot. If I'm not back by tomorrow morning, send the sheriff out after me. But not before then. Understand?" Jim looked at Barlow hard. He understood.

"Good." He left and headed for the livery stable. Hamlet stood in his stall patiently chewing on hay.

"Come on, Hamlet," Jim said, leading him out of the stall. "We're going on a ride." He looked in the stable. "Boy!" he called, remembering the young man who had questioned him last night.

"Who the hell are you calling boy?" said a burly, red-faced man with incredibly curly orange hair, wiping coffee from his upper lip. "Jim Steel?" he said. "Is that you? I heard you was in town."

Jim smiled. "Can't talk now, Curly. I need an extra horse, saddle, and double saddlebags."

"Sure, Jim," Curly said, and the man bustled, getting the horse and gear ready. "You want a lead rope, too?" he asked.

"Yes," Jim answered, then studied the saddlebags. "These things have got to look like they're weighted down. Got anything around here that might work?"

"Got just the thing," Curly said, after a short think. He disappeared as Jim put his saddle on Hamlet and fastened it. When Curly returned, he held several iron bars.

"These should do the trick," he said.

The iron bars weighted down the bags, but it was obvious that only the bottom of each bag was full. Jim looked around the place and found some pieces of wood and tucked them in, making it look, he hoped, like the double saddlebags were full to the brim with gold, two hundred pounds of gold.

"Mind if I ask you where you're going?" Curly asked, as Jim checked the bags one last time.

"Don't mind if you ask," Jim said, "but I won't tell you." Curly was notorious for his curiosity, but he ran the best livery stable in Denver, and Jim had absolute trust in the man. "I should be back by sundown. If not, then . . . I'm all paid up with you, right?"

Curly nodded. "Hell, you damn near support this place, Jim."

"Then I'll see you later, Curly," Jim said, and climbed onto Hamlet. He let the buckskin have one last drink, while he took the lead rope from the other horse and tied it onto his saddle. He then rode out of the stable into the blinding early morning sun, patting Hamlet's neck.

"Good boy," he said, as they walked into the street.

When they reached the outskirts of town, Jim was anxious to ride hard, but he knew not to. A run like that would tire Hamlet needlessly, and leave a telltale line of dust that would tip off whoever was holding Margarita. He had plenty of time.

His only concern was how many men he would be up against. Jim was pretty sure Zeke and Rufus were involved, but if they'd hired some guys in Denver, Jim was in for a real fight.

Jim discarded the idea as he rode. No, they'd

been in Denver for only a few hours; it would have taken longer than that to get some good men. And they probably would have asked for more gold, if it was to be split among many men.

Jim knew he was taking a risk riding there without the gold, but he hoped his preparations would fool the kidnappers long enough for him to get the upper hand. If he could get to the spring before the kidnapper, he could either follow him back, or beat the truth out of him. He was sure they wouldn't be stupid enough to show up with Margarita, and that they were probably planning to deliver another message later, with further instructions. That meant that he'd have to look for her. They'd have her safely hidden somewhere, probably not far away.

Jim headed south, toward the spring, keeping the sun on his left shoulder. The countryside just outside Denver was thickly forested with cottonwoods and maples. Here and there, a barren spot stood out like a hawk against the sky, but for the most part, the area was covered with trees.

He kept Hamlet at a steady canter. He'd make the five miles in less than an hour. Jim wasn't in a hurry, but he did want to get to Clearwater Spring before the kidnappers. Even though it couldn't be past eight in the morning, he had to get to the spot quickly, so that he would be there first and have the advantage.

Jim stopped at the base of the cliff he'd been watching for some time. It jutted up sharply from the wooded floor, and a twin peak lay close to it on the other side. Jim knew there was a trail leading up the closest small mountain.

He started on it, letting Hamlet pick his way. It was an old Indian path, long ago abandoned. Through years of neglect, it had nearly been covered with new growth, mostly columbines and buttercups, but there were enough traces left to mark it. Hamlet followed the trail naturally, as it was the easiest way up the hill.

The wind blew hard as they reached the top. Jim tied up Hamlet and the other horse in the shady grove of trees where some sweet grass grew, and made his way to the other side of the peak. There, at the edge of the brush, he lay on the ground and inched his way forward. After a few minutes of this painstaking work, Jim was rewarded with a view of the land on the other side of the hill — Clearwater Spring and vicinity.

The spring sat between the two sheer cliffs, one of which Jim lay on. Indians used to say that the thunder-god had split the mountain in two, after a Cheyenne chief had been killed there in battle. Though the spring had long been Sacred to the Cheyenne, they seldom used now; the Indians had been driven back, away from Denver and the surrounding areas. Now the spring was a favorite watering spot for travellers to or from Denver.

As Jim searched the lush green area below him, the trees, including a few white firs and Douglas spruce, bent in the wind, filling his ears with the sound of breaking surf. Nothing moved down there in the valley. Satisfied, he continued his visual search of the surrounding area. It seemed he had gotten there first, and hopefully, if they were on their way, they hadn't noticed his approach.

He knew that there were numerous hiding spots on the cliffs, and that a man could stay in them and never be seen, but Jim felt that he was alone. It couldn't be much before nine, so he had a good three hours until he was supposed to deliver the gold. The kidnappers were probably close by, but not within spitting distance.

Jim searched the area once more and saw nothing. There was no strange patch of color, that could be a sleeve or leg, or gleam that marked a gun barrel, and he didn't see a horse. The place was deserted.

He had hoped for it; in fact, he had expected it. Now all he had to do was wait, and hope that he saw the men before they saw him.

Margarita strained against her bonds as she sat in the corner of the dirty cabin. The ropes cut into her delicate wrists, marking them with red lines, and the gag that had been tied around her mouth nearly choked her. She had never felt so dirty, helpless, and humiliated.

The men hadn't touched her, it was true — at least, not in the way that she feared they might. But they had kidnapped her, and taken her to the cabin. She couldn't quite remember now what had happened, and had no recollection of the trip there; she must have passed out. But she had woken up lying on a dirty mattress in the corner of a cabin, staring up at two men.

Margarita had been surprised when she saw her captor's face. It was Zeke Slade, who had been with the exhibition from the beginning. What could he possibly hope to accomplish by this outrageous act?

Margarita comforted herself by thinking that Zeke was not the type of person who would harm her. At least, he hadn't seemed that type of person. He was artistic and intelligent, to a certain degree — he had to be, to do the kind of work he had done on the exhibition's touring train car. He wasn't the criminal sort of person at all.

But the other man — she had heard Zeke call him Rufus — wasn't to be trusted. Rufus stared at her constantly, making lewd comments and reaching out, as if to touch her. Each time, Margarita had pressed her back to the wall, and so far, Zeke had managed to stop Rufus from carrying out his threats. Margarita hoped that Zeke wouldn't leave her. Though he had kidnapped her, she realized that he was also protecting her.

She wondered how long she had sat in the corner. It had been light for hours and the men had made a breakfast of coffee, bacon, and bread long ago. She had been revolted by Rufus's eating habits, but found herself getting hungry while she watched the men eat.

She couldn't ask for food, even if she had wanted to; the gag was thoroughly effective, and when she tried to speak, Rufus would mock her futile attempts. She gave that up after a few tries.

Zeke walked up to her.

"Margarita," he said. "I hope you realize that I don't like doing this to you, and I can assure you that no harm will come to you, if Jim Steel does what I told him to do. I'm sorry you had to be involved this way, but you were the only choice." He looked at her coldly for a moment, then turned away.

The look on Zeke's face chilled her. Despite what he had said about not hurting her, Margarita wondered. Why shouldn't he hurt her? She wondered what the penalty was for kidnapping. Probably hanging, she thought with a shudder. So he had nothing to lose!

She wished that she were free of her bonds. If the gag were off, she could talk to Zeke, perhaps reason with him. He wasn't unintelligent. Maybe she could talk him out of this thing that he was doing.

Every time she thought about it, however, she saw Rufus's face, the disgusting lips, the eyes consumed with lust, and her courage failed her.

"What time is it?" Rufus asked.

Zeke pulled out his pocket watch. "Ten-thirty," he said. "Still early."

"Maybe you should ride out, and check to see if he's there yet," Rufus suggested.

"No, I don't think that's necessary. He'll be busy scrambling around trying to get that gold together. With Barlow's contacts, I can't see him having too many problems, though; after all, the Denver Mint's right there." Zeke smiled at the thought. "Maybe I should have asked for more. But no matter. What's done is done."

Margarita listened to their conversation with interest. Apparently, they had asked Jim Steel to give them some gold, probably in exchange for her. A doubt came to her mind; would Jim arrange for the gold to be delivered? Of course, he would, she thought. Then they would let her go, and she would try to forget the whole terrifying experience.

But would they let her go? Margarita forced herself to remain calm and poised. Once they had the gold, who said they had to give her back to Jim Steel? She would be a burden, true; and they would probably want to get away quickly, and wouldn't want to bring her along. There was another possibility, but she refused to consider it. She had to maintain her composure as far as possible under the circumstances.

"I gotta say," Rufus said, "you sure pulled this one off good, like a real pro."

Zeke spread out his hands. "All it takes is thinking, Rufus," he said. "Most guys try to commit crimes, like robbery, without using their heads. You've got to move fast, hit them where they'll least likely be expectin' it, and then clear out just as fast. Outsmart them, the men who're paid to take you in, like Jim Steel," he said. "That's the secret." Then he turned to look at Margarita. "And of course, it helps to have a beautiful woman involved as well," Zeke said, and then laughed.

Rufus joined in, looking at Margarita.

For the first time since she'd been captured, Margarita welcomed the gag. Without it, she was sure she would have screamed.

Chapter Eight

Jim waited in stoic silence. The sun had slicked his skin, making his clothes feel heavy and uncomfortable. But he lay still on top of the cliff, above the spring, watching. Once he caught himself dozing, but woke up quickly, not wanting to miss anything.

A few times, he was startled by a deer or rabbit scampering through the brush. Aside from an occasional animal, however, he was quite alone. Jim heard Hamlet nicker once and then fall silent, but he knew he didn't have to check on his buckskin. Hamlet would let him know if anything happened to him.

Jim carefully rolled over, laying his rifle on the ground beside him. Reaching into his pocket, he pulled out his pocket watch. Five minutes until twelve. He wound it, and then slipped it back into his pocket. As he rolled onto his stomach, he saw something.

Far in the distance, a tiny beige line extended up from the ground. It lay in the east, where the land was barren; few trees grew there and the area was dry and deserted. Even the Indians had avoided it, saying it had been cursed by the gods, Jim remembered someone once telling him. Now a rider, alone by the looks of the dust trail, crossed that expanse. He was heading in Jim's direction.

Jim wished he had the field glasses he had used in the army. He liked the idea of seeing who was coming before they saw him. But he'd have to be patient, and wait until the rider was closer. Jim was well hidden, so the man couldn't see him.

Jim reconsidered his plan. If the man rode up and didn't see Jim there, or the gold, he'd either ride back or start snooping around. Jim didn't want that. No, he'd better make it look like he'd been there already. Judging from the lengthening brown streak of the dust trail in the sky, Jim figured that he had about ten minutes before the rider reached the spring. He slid back from the cliff, still taking every precaution, and went to the horses.

He took the extra horse and led him down the trail on the back of the cliff. At the spring, he tied the animal to a tree, then took a quick drink, clearing the dust from his throat with the gloriously cold clear water that bubbled up from beneath a rock. He splashed some over his head, put his hat back on, and then started up the trail. Jim hurried as he climbed, knowing the man would be there soon. It had taken him longer than he had expected to lead the horse down the trail, and he'd used up precious moments at the spring.

Soon he was back on top of the cliff, in front of the bush he'd been using for cover, his rifle resting easy in a notched rock that looked as if it had been placed there for just that purpose.

Jim had a clear view and line of fire for the whole valley. He had deliberately positioned the horse with the stuffed saddlebags so that it was it the nearest point in the valley to him, not more than two hundred feet away. Now he waited.

A minute later, a horse snorted somewhere below him. It was tired, and complaining to its rider.

"Easy, Nelly," a man said.

Jim listened closely to the voice. He couldn't put a face or name to it, but it seemed familiar.

Moments later, Zeke Slade, his face unshaven and dirty, rode into the protected valley of Clear-water Spring. He stared at the horse with the bulging saddlebags that Jim had placed near the spring.

"Yep, that Jim Steel sure knows how to follow instructions. He even left me a horse to take it back on. He'd never do anything to hurt Margarita, right, Nelly?" Zeke said.

Zeke dismounted and walked to the spring. Just before he got there, however, Zeke turned and listened to the wind, then looked up at the cliffs on both sides of him.

"Funny he didn't stick around, ain't it, Nelly?" he said to the horse.

He knows I'm here, Jim thought. Zeke studied the ground, found Jim's footprints, and began to follow them. Jim decided to hurry along the inevitable.

He fired a warning shot, not wanting to kill the man — not yet, anyway.

Zeke swung low, then crouched behind a bush that grew near the spring. He looked up at the cliff, watching the blue smoke from the powder fade into the air.

"Who's there?" he said, his voice shaky but loud.

Jim was silent. He moved four yards laterally along the cliff. If he killed Zeke, he might not find Margarita. If Zeke got away, there was a chance that Jim would lose his trail.

"I said, who's there? That you, Jim Steel?" Zeke said, his head bobbing from behind the bush, looking around the valley as if crazed by bad whiskey.

Jim lay still, keeping the bush in his rifle sight. But he wasn t ready for the man's next move.

A slug exploded a rock not far from Jim's head. Several fragments hit his hair, but did no damage. When he got the bush in his sight again, it was still; apparently, Zeke had moved. Where could he have gone? Jim picked up the man's image again, not more than four feet from where he had been, bent at the waist, and moving to his horse behind the meager cover of patches of brush.

Jim fired another shot and heard a scream. Zeke stood upright, holding his chest. Blood showed on the man's shirt, and he yelled again.

Jim scrambled to the edge of the cliff, and, taking the short way down, stopped onto the steep slope. He kept one eye on Zeke as he ran nimbly down the cliff, dodged around a pine tree, and stopped, his rifle aimed at Zeke.

The man stood in the clean sand beside the spring.

"Steel," he said as Jim walked up.

"Where's Margarita?" Jim asked. "And what about that bomb in the train car?"

"If you think I'm going to tell you anything, you've got —"

"You want to die out here alone?" Jim asked, wondering how he had shot the man in the chest. He'd been aiming for the right arm; Zeke must have moved faster, or slower, than Jim had allowed for.

Zeke fell to his knees. A trickle of blood oozed out between his lips; he tasted it, recognized it, and his eyes widened.

"Where's Margarita?" Jim asked again, standing over the man.

Zeke moaned and slid to the ground. His lips pursed, as if trying to say something, and then his head rolled to one side. The right foot jerked once and was still. Jim watched Zeke Slade slowly, silently, die.

Jim stared down at the body, and then headed back to the trail up the other side of the cliff. Nothing he could do now, except backtrack the man, head to where he had come from. The sandy area should have left clear prints.

Jim went to Hamlet and took him down to the spring. After thinking for a moment, Jim took the saddlebags and put them on Hamlet. He then tied a rope from Hamlet to lead Zeke's horse, bent to take the hat off the dead man's head, and tied that onto his saddle. Jim let the two horses have a drink before he headed east, leaving the third horse at the spring.

The trail was easy to follow as soon as Jim was clear of the brush and trees. The soft sand had left clean hoofprints.

A half-hour later, the barren land ended, at the edge of a stream. The lush greenery around the stream meant that it was a year-round river. At the wooded area's edge, Jim thought he had lost the tracks, but picked them up again. Torn leaves and hoofprints on the mulch that lay under the big trees left a clear trail.

The tracks turned abruptly into the shallow stream, and sure enough, the bank where he stood was wet. It must have marked where Zeke had come out of the water. Jim crossed the stream and took up the trail on the other side, wondering what he'd find at its end.

Rufus Jackson was the other missing man. Jim guessed he'd find Rufus and Margarita in an abandoned mine, or maybe an old miner's cabin. Colorado was littered with them, especially near streams.

He'd decide how to handle it once he got there, though he knew part of what he'd do. He kept his eyes open and searching for anything that might help him discover where they were, for he had to make preparations before he was seen.

At last, at about one o'clock, he saw a cabin in the distance. Though the area around it had been cleared some years ago, new trees, six and seven feet tall, had sprung up around the old trunk, telling Jim that the cabin had been deserted for several years. Had a miner been living there still he would have kept it cleared. It was possible that that was where Rufus was holding Margarita.

Jim stopped the horses behind a few trees, then dismounted and hid his hat under a bush. He marked the place with crossed branches on the ground. He then put on Zeke's hat, got on Zeke's horse, tied Hamlet to lead him, and rode toward the cabin.

As he neared it, he saw two horses tied up on the side. When he was fifty feet away from the structure, the door opened. Jim kept his head down, showing off the horse and hat to full advantage.

"You got it?" a voice said from inside the cabin, though Jim didn't look to see its owner.

Jim nodded. "Yep." He tried to say it as much like Zeke as he could.

"Why're you lookin' so down, then?" the voice said. "Wait a minute."

Jim chanced a look up. Rufus Jackson stood in the doorway, in full view.

"You ain't Zeke!" he said.

Jim swung his .45 up and fired, blasting a slug through the cabin window inches from Rufus. If he'd had time to aim, it would have hit its mark.

Rufus ducked back inside the cabin as the costly window shattered, cursing louder than the smashing glass could drown out. Jim jumped off the horse, tied them both up to a tree so they wouldn't run off, then hid behind a Colorado oak.

A shot burst out from the cabin, striking a nearby bush. Jim shot into the air, over the cabin, remembering that Margarita was probably inside. He didn't want to risk firing into the cabin and hitting her. He bent and ran to another tree, knowing the thick blue smoke would give away his location.

More shots sounded through the trees, as Jim moved from trunk to trunk, crisscrossing the area, trying to confuse Rufus. Jim fired twice more, each time from different areas, but he saved his last few bullets for important work.

Jim made his way around the back of the cabin without Rufus following his movements. There, looking from behind a tree, he could see through a window. Rufus was on the floor, his back to Jim, reloading his sixgun. Jim crouched, then ran to the window. As Rufus shot another round into the trees, Jim aimed and fired through the glass. The bullet struck Rufus's right hand, spinning the sixgun to the dirt floor.

Rufus turned in surprise, then looked at his weapon.

"Don't try for it," Jim said.

Rufus reached for the gun.

"You'll never make it," Jim said quietly.

"Hell," Rufus said.

"Stand up."

The man did so. Jim kicked out the remains of the window he'd fired through and jumped inside the cabin. As soon as he was inside, he realized that something was missing.

"Where's Margarita?"

Rufus stared at Jim's .45.

"You gonna kill me?" Rufus asked.

"Where's the girl?" Jim asked menacingly.

"Oh, she run off."

"Where? And when?"

"Not long ago, just before you got here."

"Where'd she go?" Jim asked, wondering if the man were lying.

"I don't know. I was too busy a-pullin' my pants up, if you know what I mean." Rufus smiled.

Jim ignored his comment. He didn't know what to do with Rufus. Obviously, he'd have to go out looking for Margarita, but he didn't want to kill the man. Besides, there was one more question that needed to be answered, before he went looking for Margarita.

"About that bomb in the train car," Jim said. "How do we defuse it, and where is it hidden?"

Rufus laughed. "You mean he done fooled you with that?" The man snorted. "Hell, he told me he tried that trick twice before, and it never worked."

"You mean, there's no bomb?" Jim asked.

"Hell, no."

Jim accepted the fact. Now he had other things to think about.

"Sit down," he said, pointing to a chair.

Reluctantly Rufus moved to it, dropping his cheery mood. Jim moved behind him, found a piece of rope, and tied the man securely to the chair.

"You gonna leave me here to die?" Rufus asked.

"No. The sheriff'll be along soon enough to take you to jail." Jim checked over the knots, decided all were fast, and stood.

"You telling me the truth about Margarita and the bomb?" Jim asked.

"On the Bible," Rufus said. "Zeke told me he'd tried that bomb thing before, and it never worked. He threw it in at the last minute to scare you guys more. And he also told me not to fool around with Margarita, but I figured when he was gone collectin' the gold, I'd have a try . . . and she got away."

"Alright," Jim said, and left the cabin.

He got up on Hamlet, tied Zeke's horse onto his, and retrieved his hat, throwing Zeke's on the ground. Now, where would a woman go, in the middle of the woods, scared half out of her mind?

She'd probably hear the water and go to the stream, thinking it would lead to a town. Would she follow it upstream, or down? Jim thought, and decided that she probably knew that most towns lay downstream.

Jim took the horse to the stream, and sure enough, he picked up someone's trail. A piece of white cloth lay on the ground, next to some clear impressions of small naked feet.

He continued following the trail next to the stream, walking beside the horses now, because he knew she couldn't have gone far.

"Margarita?" he called out. "It's Jim Steel. Where are you?"

The trail ended suddenly. It didn't veer off to the river, nor did it turn away. It simply stopped. Where had the fool woman gone?

Jim heard a wimper above him. He looked up and saw a form, huddled against a branch, perched in a giant, ancient oak. Margarita Contreras, niece of the Mexican president, Jim thought, sitting in a tree.

"Margarita," he said.

The woman didn't seem to hear him.

"Margarita, it's me, Jim Steel."

"Get away from me, Rufus," she said, her voice vicious but tired.

"It's not Rufus. It's really me, Jim. Take a look."

Her head turned reluctantly. The hair, which had been so beautifully arranged for their dinner the night before, was matted with dirt and mud; leaves stuck out from the once-intricate ringlets. Tears sprang from her eyes, as she looked and saw him standing below her.

"Jim!" she said. Forgetting that she was in a tree, she reached out for him and fell.

Jim caught her before she had a chance to scream. Looking at her, even though she was scratched and dirty, Jim knew she was one of the most beautiful women he'd ever seen.

"Where have you been?" she said, scolding him. "If you knew what that filthy Rufus Jackson tried to do . . ." she began, and then stopped. Margarita looked down at herself unhappily. "I need a bath."

Jim laughed. "At least you're alive and safe," he said, and started to put her down.

But at that moment, Margarita reached up, touched his cheek and kissed it.

"Thank you, Jim Steel," she said.

He sat her on Zeke's horse, not telling her who its former owner was, and then mounted Hamlet. He led her gently along the stream, stopped to check on Rufus, who had fallen asleep on the chair, and then cut across the river to go to the spring. There, while the horses drank and he tied the horse he had left there onto Hamlet, Margarita walked up to him. She hadn't mentioned Zeke's body, which lay in full view on the sand.

"I had a feeling about him," she said, looking at the prone figure.

"About Zeke?" Jim asked, looking up from his impromptu rubdown on Hamlet.

"Yes, Zeke and Rufus. They never did strike me as being very honest men," she said, pulling sticks out of her hair.

Jim smiled. "Then why didn't you tell me?"

"Why didn't I tell you?" she said, and then looked at Jim incredulously. "I told you over and over, remember? I must have said it three dozen times. I —"

Jim cut off her sentence by taking her in his arms and pressing his lips to hers. Margarita struggled at first, but soon gave in to the kiss.

"And that's another thing," she began, as he lifted his mouth from hers.

"Save it for later," he said, and helped Margarita onto Zeke's horse. "We've still got a long ride ahead of us."

"I won't ride this way again," she said. "I'll only ride sidesaddle."

"Sorry," Jim said. "But you can't ride sidesaddle without that kind of saddle. It's impossible."

"Don't tell me it's impossible," she said, and struggled to get both legs on the same side of the horn. After a few attempts, she gave up, exhausted.

"Manners and niceties are for the big city," Jim said, mounting Hamlet. "Out here, you just do the job the way it has to be done, no matter how. We've got to get back to Denver, and you've got to ride that horse. Those are facts. So let's go."

Margarita glared at him, but she tried to make herself comfortable.

"I'll get even with you for this, Jim Steel," she said, as they began riding.

He laughed. Margarita Contreras hadn't changed.

Chapter Nine

The exhibition in Denver came off without any more problems. Rufus was jailed, and after six days, Margarita decided it was time to move on.

Jim had watched with growing uneasiness the strained relationship between Margarita and Rafael Romero. He knew that Romero hated her for taking over his job, and the girl seemed to return his dislike. It didn't make any sense, but Jim knew that it could lead to trouble if he let it get out of hand. That's one thing they didn't need more of — trouble. They'd already had their share of that on this tour.

Jim sat watching the scenery go by outside the window. Every spare moment of his time was taken up with thoughts about the tour, security, and the personnel involved. So far he'd been able to handle the problems that came up. From now on, he'd have to stop them before they became problems.

He'd have to take stronger measures to ensure that the gold wasn't stolen. Jim decided to spend each night in the exhibit car. There was enough room to lay out a bedroll on the floor. That way anybody who wanted to get the gold would have to step over him, and Jim was an Indian sleeper. The slightest noise and he was wide awake, with his .45 drawn and ready.

Jim glanced at Margarita Contreras. She hadn't

changed much since her kidnapping; perhaps she acted a bit kinder towards Jim, more considerate. But that hadn't changed her views about his fitness for the job, or her worries about security. Nor had it made her grow fonder of Romero.

Jim caught the two arguing four times on the trip to Sacramento. Each time he had warned them to settle their differences and to get along together, but both parties had always walked off in silence to brood somewhere else.

Maybe it would be a good idea to talk with Margarita about that now, Jim thought. He got up and walked down the aisle, then stood beside the young woman's chair.

"Margarita?" he said.

"Yes?" The young woman turned her head and smiled slightly.

"There's something I want to talk to you about."

"I see," she said, and turned to her duenna. A moment later, Tia Rosa rose from where she had been sitting beside Margarita and moved to another seat. Then Margarita moved over next to the window and Jim sat beside her.

Just as Jim was about to speak, Margarita raised her hand to silence him.

"If this is about Rafael Romero, I have nothing to say," she said.

"Nothing?" Jim asked.

"That is correct."

"You mean you're not fighting with him anymore?" he asked, knowing that wasn't what the young woman meant, but wanting her to pursue the subject further.

"Well," she said, and then paused. "I am no longer talking with Rafael Romero. We have nothing further to discuss, so what is the use? It only angers us both. We have come to an agreement that we will not discuss the problem again. And since that is the only thing we have discussed for the past several weeks, there is nothing left to talk about. So that is what I meant."

Jim shook his head. Margarita was an interesting girl. If only she were grown up, and made more sense.

"Alright," he said. "The only reason I wanted to talk to you about Romero was because your fights have been affecting other people on the tour. You've got everyone's tempers high and I don't like that. So no more fighting in front of other people, alright?"

"Mr. Steel," she said. "I already told you that there will be no more arguments between Rafael and I. Is that understood?"

"Yes," Jim said.

"When I give my word, I keep it. You have nothing to worry about." Margarita stared at him levelly, her gaze cold. But as she continued to look at Jim, it softened again. Her eyelids fluttered again. "I am sorry," she said. "It is just that this tour has affected me. I do not think that I will be myself until the artifacts are safely back in my country. The tour has been a huge strain on me. If it shows, if I have acted less than polite,

I am sorry." She looked away from Jim. "I did not mean to."

Jim nodded. "I understand."

She looked at him. "You do? I hope so. I don't think that I have recovered from the night when Zeke Slade and that other man — I've forgotten his name — took me from my hotel room to that cabin." She shuddered. "I've never had anything like that happen to me. I'm so grateful that you came and found me the way you did. Otherwise I might still be in that forest, looking for Denver."

Jim remembered how she looked that day; dirty hair and face, her nightgown and robe torn and tattered, her feet bare. But even then she had been beautiful, and was much more so now, seven days later, sitting on the train bound for Sacramento.

He realized that he had been staring at her.

"Something wrong, Jim?" Margarita asked, as she saw him looking at her.

"No," he said. "Nothing at all. I was just thinking about the whole thing — the kidnapping and everything else. I never thought anyone would have the gall to try that." He shook his head.

"I can see why they did," Margarita said. "It was much more effective than if they had taken a man . . . Romero, for instance," she said.

"Yes, that's true," Jim said. "But that's not what I meant. Women are nearly sacred in the West. Why, they can do nearly anything and the men won't mind, as long as they don't hurt themselves or anyone else. No, ma'am, there's too few women in the West for any man to mistreat them, like Zeke and Rufus did you. Course, frustration sometimes drives a man to madness, which is what looks like happened to them."

Margarita shook her shoulders gently. "The fact remains that they did. But I would rather not talk about it," she said. "If you would not mind, there is something which I must discuss with Tia Rosa."

Jim nodded and rose. "Right. I'll see you later." He moved back to his seat as Tia Rosa resumed her place beside Margarita. One of these days, Jim thought, I'm going to understand Margarita. He laughed and looked outside the window, watching the heavy timbered slopes of the Rocky Mountains slide by.

Rafael Romero frowned. He hadn't smiled since Margarita Contreras had taken over his job directing the tour of Aztecan artifacts from the Mexico City Museum of Culture to the United States. One moment, he was preparing, arranging, cataloging . . . and the next, some young upstart woman who happened to be the president's niece walked in and said she was taking over. The girl's attitude, while friendly on the surface, began to grate on him after a day or two. He hadn't shown it then, but it became increasingly hard to hide it over the weeks. Now it positively infuriated him, and he didn't try hiding it anymore.

Romero drove his fist into the cushion of the empty seat beside him. He couldn't put up with much more. The woman was bothering him endlessly. Even though they had told each other they wouldn't confront one another again about the problem, he still thought about it day and night. It would not leave him.

He had worked at the museum, studying the ancient civilizations of Mexico for twenty years, devoting his life to his work. And now, in what should have been his moment of greatest triumph and satisfaction, displaying the fruits of his labor, research, and sweat to the United States, he stood in the shadow of a girl young enough to be his daughter.

It wasn't fair, he told himself. He wouldn't let her receive all the credit. No. He'd have to do something to bring his name out, to glorify Rafael Romero for all time, in both the United States and Mexico.

But what could he do? Romero couldn't think of a thing. Margarita would share time talking with the people about the artifacts and the purpose of the tour, but she was sure to take more time than she gave him, maybe two hours to his half-hour. What could he do in that time?

It would have to be something else, something so spectacular that even Margarita Contreras would be speechless, and quite possibly, thankful.

What a feeling that would be, Romero decided, as a wave of emotion swept through him. What a triumphant moment! He would work toward it, make it a reality. But what could bring it about? What could he do?

Romero thought for over an hour, as they rolled toward Sacramento. Finally he shook his head. No, he was thinking along the wrong lines. There must be an easier way to capture that glory. He knew there was, but it wouldn't come to him. Not at the moment, at least. But it would come.

He could practically feel Margarita breathing down his neck, though she sat several rows behind him. The woman had taken total control over the tour; that much he could say for her. And she hadn't done a bad job. But the only reason that she had gotten the position was that she was the president's niece. Rafael Romero was far better qualified, more experience, and more suited to the directorship of the tour. But all this had been forgotten when the black-haired girl who had always wanted to lead an exhibition to the United States came along.

Romero felt his anger surge again; he pressed his fist to the seat until his knuckles turned white. Then, with an effort, he let the rage slip back inside him. He sighed and stared out the window.

The idea would come. He knew it would. And when it did, Rafael Romero would be ready for it.

They arrived in Sacramento without further problems, stopping on a siding as close to the business section of the city as possible, amid much curiosity. The *Sacramento Bee* had run a story on the exhibit, saying they were on their way. Margarita found she didn't have to drum up any interest; all of Sacramento, it seemed, wanted to see the exhibit. This pleased her, and she urged the men to get everything set up quickly, so that the exhibit could open.

Jim went over new schedules for his security force and laid out positioning of his men. In each city, it had to be different, taking into account the buildings, streets, and other factors. Jim made it as difficult as possible for a person to get the gold in the first place, then to move away from the car with it, and finally to run down one of the streets that led from the car. The three-layer security system had worked so far, and Jim didn't forsee any problems.

Now that they were in Sacramento, Jim decided to put into action his plan to spend the nights in the car. He'd go there every night, and then just at sunrise, he'd get up and go back to his hotel room, shave, and come back. It was like working round-the-clock, but Jim didn't mind. He would rather give up comforts than see the gold stolen; too many people were depending on him to safeguard the exhibit. And he'd do just that, as far as he could.

Jim decided not to ask Margarita out to dinner in Sacramento. Not that he wouldn't mind, but he knew he'd never be able to get her alone, without Tia Rosa. The thought of another dinner with the older woman along, watching Jim's every move and weighing his words, was enough to make him hold off another invitation.

He was sure that if he could get Margarita alone, she'd open up to him and become the warm, vulnerable girl that she was in reality. But that would take time and luck, Jim thought. He wasn't worried; they still had more than a month on the tour for him to work on the problem.

Perhaps he'd ask her tomorrow, he thought, as he chewed a delicious piece of steak at the dining table in his hotel. Hell, she'd probably just say no, but at least he would have asked her. The more Jim thought about it, the more he smiled. Tia Rosa had never cut him down; she'd never interrupted his conversations with Margarita, never shown the slightest dislike for him. Maybe if he moved cautiously, he could gain her trust and she'd leave them alone together. It would be well worth the wait, Jim thought, with a grin.

He finished his dinner, wiped his mouth, and picked up the bedroll he'd made up in his room. It was nearly sundown. He wanted to get to the car by dusk, when the most dangerous part of the security man's life began. Half the whole two-month long tour took place at night, and during that time, the chances of someone stealing the gold were highest, At night there were fewer people around, and guards got tired. He walked to the car swiftly. As he approached it, Jim remembered that he hadn't told anyone that he planned to spend the night there. So much the better, he thought, as he balanced the bedroll on his shoulder.

"Mr Steel!" one of the guards called as Jim walked up to the train car. "Something wrong?"

"No," he said. "Just felt like sleeping in the car tonight. Wake me up at sunrise," he said, unlocking the door.

"I only work until six," the man said. "But I can have Simpson — he's the guy who relieves me — do it, if you want."

"Good," Jim said. "Tell him sunrise. Just bang on the door. It'll be locked."

"Yes, sir," the guard said. "I'll tell him."

Jim climbed up the steps and unlocked the door, then walked in and locked the door. The car was cool and quiet — and pitch black. Jim laid the bedroll down in the area in front of the glassed-in display case. Fortunately, there was lots of room for Jim to sprawl his taller-than-average frame, and he got comfortable quickly.

The night was quiet. Jim heard one of his guards whistling; it was a tune he hadn't heard in years. Some girl in a New York opera house had sung it. He knew he should get up and tell the man to be quiet, but Jim felt exhaustion set in, and he soon closed his eyes.

Romero peered from behind the wagon. Steel had placed five guards around the train car tonight. Damn. One could never tell in advance how many he'd use. Romero was glad that he'd hired ten men; he would need them, and it would give him two men per guard.

Romero turned back to the men, who stood in the alley next to the two wagons they brought. Two of the men kept the horses quiet, and the others stood, eyes forward, ready for action. One man, with a huge, ugly scar over his right eye, slid the barrel of his .45 along his ear impatiently.

"Remember," Romero said to the men, looking hard at the gun-toting one. "Don't fire a shot unless absolutely necessary. We don't want to wake up the rest of the city. That'll ruin our plans. There're five guards out there, so you'll have two men per guard. No killing, as I told you before. Just knock them out, and do it so it won't make the other guards suspicious. No, they can't see each other. Alright," Romero said, feeling sweat break out on his forehead. "You two, go for the first guard. He's leaning against that door closest to us. Go!" he said in his thick Spanish accent.

The two men slid along like shadows, creeping up on the closest guard from opposite sides. One of them stood directly behind him and cupped his hand over the man's mouth. Before the guard could struggle much, the second man knocked him on the head, and the guard slumped to the ground. The men dragged him away and tied him up.

The next two men were dispatched by Romero as soon as the first couple were finished. They did their work quickly, so Romero let the others go, coming at the guards on all sides, silently, slowly. Soon all five guards were unconscious. They'd have large headaches when they woke up, Romero thought smugly, but they wouldn't be permanently damaged.

Romero led the first wagon up to the rail car, then stepped up onto the metal stairs leading to the door. He slid his key into the lock and gently opened the door.

At that moment, he saw a man standing in front of him inside the car.

Romero froze. What was happening? Who was it?

"Who are you?" the darkened figure said.

After a moment, the Mexican's eyes adjusted to the darkness.

"Oh, it's you, Mr. Steel," he said. His mind raced; how could he explain this to the security man? He felt the man with the scar step up on the stairs behind him. He must have done that to see what was happening.

"These men have taken me as a prisoner," Romero said quickly, thinking of each word as he said it. "They forced me to open the door, so they could get to the gold. I'm —"

Romero didn't have to finish the sentence. Before Jim could react, the scarred man reached past the Mexican and brought the butt of his pistol down on Jim's head. His eyes glazed over slightly, and then he sank to the ground.

"Good work," Romero said, wiping the sweat from his face. "We've got to tie him up to make sure he won't get in the way again."

The man got a length of rope from one of the wagons and tied the security man firmly, then pushed Jim's limp body into the corner.

Romero quickly removed one of the glass panels of the display by stripping off the molding, and then lifting out the pane. His excitement rose; he saw the gold glisten dully in the moonlight that came in from the opened door. So far, everything had happened according to schedule. Even Jim Steel's unexpected appearance inside the car hadn't altered the plan.

Romero now began handing the larger gold statues out. They went by way of a human chain of hands into the wagon. The last man gently laid each one down on the thick folds of blankets and mattresses that Romero had put there to protect the pieces from damage.

After one layer was filled, the man stopped the chain momentarily to lay down another protective covering for the next batch of artifacts.

When that wagon had been filled, they began loading the second. Romero concentrated on the larger pieces; they were easier to handle, and were less likely to break or be damaged in transit. At several intervals, he whispered out to his men to be careful with the objects.

Nearly an hour after he had first looked over the guards from the alley, they were finished. All the larger gold pieces were gone. Now they had to leave before it got light. Besides, Romero wasn't too sure when the guards and Jim Steel would wake up, and the next shift would be coming on soon. He didn't want to be there when the guards arrived.

He left the car, closed and locked the door and then rode off on one of the wagons with the rest of the men on horseback. They had carried out his perfect plan, he thought. Nothing had gone wrong! Nothing could go wrong. He felt pride swell up inside him. All this for his own glory; no, for his own right to glory. This wouldn't be necessary if Margarita hadn't . . . Romero smiled. It didn't matter now. It had been done. All he had to do was pay off his men, then haul the artifacts back into town, with a wild story about how they had kidnapped him and forced him to open the train car door, which was something Jim Steel would back him up on. After they had taken the artifacts, he'd tell them, they took him as a hostage, tied him up, and threw him in the back of one of the wagons. Through his own ingenuity, he finally escaped and brought the gold back with him. They would believe the story, simply because Jim Steel backed him up on it, and he would tell it so well no one would doubt him. Everyone would be relieved to have the artifacts back, as well.

Romero bundled his coat up around him as he thought of the honor he would receive. The night air was cold as they rode south out of Sacramento, but inside he felt warm, knowing that he would, at last, get the attention that he deserved, after devoting his entire life to those artifacts.

He laughed as he thought of Jim Steel lying tied up and unconscious in the train car. He had always thought the man wasn't good enough to head their security!

Chapter Ten

"Hey! What's going on here? Where the hell is everybody?"

Jim heard the voice dimly as it came from outside the train car. He opened his eyes and instantly the pain on the top of his head intensified. It seemed that it was still night outside, as the inside of the car was still black. Trying to stand up, he was surprised to find his hands had been firmly tied together. He moved so that his back was to the wall, then walked up it with his hands, gradually lifting himself to his feet.

"Hey!" Jim shouted, so that whoever was outside could hear him.

"Someone in there?" the voice asked suspiciously.

"Yeah, it's Jim Steel," he said, walking to the door. "Get me the hell out of here."

"Now, do you expect me to believe that you're Jim Steel?" the man said dubiously.

"I am, dammit," Jim shouted. "Let me out."

"No. I know you ain't Jim Steel. If you was, you'd have a key and could get yourself out of there. Maybe I should go wake Mr. Steel and have him take care of you. I have to find out where the guards went to, anyway."

"If you don't get me out of here in ten seconds," Jim said, "you're out of a job, buster. I'm tied up and can't reach my key. Let me out of here. Now!"

"Well, I don't have a key." the man said. "How can I get you out of there?"

"Find one," Jim answered. He saw faint light coming from beneath the door; apparently, it was near morning. The man had probably just shown up for the day shift.

"Where can I find a key?" he asked.

"Barlow, Romero, Miss Contreras . . . they've all got keys. Track one of them down, and tell them what I told you."

"Well, alright," the man said. "I'll be back. But I still don't think you're Jim Steel."

Jim closed his eyes and leaned against the wall. He was exhausted and didn't know why. Why was he tied up? He strained to remember; it was locked somewhere inside his brain.

Then he thought about Romero coming into the train car last night. That's right. And that bigger man he had glimpsed standing behind Romero. Just when Romero was telling him what was happening, the man had knocked him out.

If they were there in the car last night, Jim thought, and they knocked him out . . . the gold! In the dim light, Jim couldn't see whether any pieces were missing from the display, but he could feel the hole where the heavy glass should have been.

Damn! Jim thought. They must have taken the gold . . . if not all of it, then some of it. He had to get out of there and get on the road to track them down. He didn't believe that they had gotten away with it. Why didn't Romero try to fight back? Maybe the man was too scared to do anything but what the thief told him to do. That museum director didn't look like the fighting kind of man.

Where the hell was that man with the key? Jim struggled, trying to loosen the knots, but they were far too snugly tied. He paced back and forth in the train car's viewing section, kicking his bedroll to one side. At least he knew about the theft; if he hadn't spent the night there, he might not have found out until much later. But then, he wouldn't have been knocked out either.

Jim cursed himself for letting the man get past him last night. There was no excuse for it, except that Jim hadn't seen the gun in the man's hand until it was striking his head; Romero's head had hidden it.

No use worrying about that now, Jim thought. There were more important things to think about. If they did move the gold, they must've used wagons to cart it out of the area. If it was light, Jim could search for the tracks in the dirt and see how how many wagons they had used. He'd then know how many men he was up against, at least approximately, and how many of his own men he would need to take with him. But he couldn't do a damn thing until he was out of the train car.

He could take his army sharpshooters — at least some of them. They'd be better, more reliable shots than the men he'd hired in St. Louis. Jim wondered if the men who'd stolen the gold had stayed together, or split up. If they had gone off in different directions, they must not have had a formal leader, unless they had already divided up the gold. That man Romero was with seemed be the leader type; maybe he had everything planned before they took the gold.

Romero, Jim thought. He'd almost forgotten the man. He wondered what the men had done with Romero. Obviously they had used him to get into the car. After that, they could have shot him, dumped him into the Sacramento river, left him tied up somewhere . . . the possibilities were endless. Jim had no great liking for Romero, but he knew he'd have to find him, although the gold was first on his list.

Where the hell was the man he'd sent to get the key? Jim paced in the car, waiting. Finally, he heard metal slide against metal, and a second later, a flood of light spilled into the car as the door swung open.

Jim instantly turned to look at the display case. He was shocked; every large piece had been taken, as well as a few of the smaller ones. More than half the gold was gone; the thieves were mainly after the big-money pieces, it seemed to Jim.

Jim heard a scream behind him. He turned to see Margarita, who had opened the door, standing in the car. She held one hand over her mouth, staring at the display area.

"We don't have time for that now," he said. "Untie my hands."

Margarita continued staring at the display in shock, unable to move or think.

"Margarita, get over here and untie my hands," Jim said, firmly and loudly. This seemed to snap her out of her spell and she turned to look at him.

"What?"

Jim showed her his hands, that were tied behind his back.

"Get me out of these, so I can get out of here and find the gold," he said.

She moved to him slowly, then ran up to Jim and slapped his face hard.

"How could you?" she said, her face twisted with anger. "I trusted you to protect that gold. And now it's all gone, and you're tied up."

"Get me out of these ropes, now," Jim said.

Grudgingly, the woman bent and began working on the ropes. "I never should have trusted you," she said. "I knew I should have gone ahead and . . ." She broke off as Jim scowled at her.

"They took Romero as hostage, or at least I think they did. They had him last night when they came in here, knocked me out, and tied me up."

"They have Señor Romero?" she said, tugging at the ropes that bound Jim's hands together.

"That's right," he said. "So I've got to find the gold and Romero. Not that I really care what happens to him."

"Mr. Steel, you'd better find the artifacts and

bring them back here," she said. Her voice was controlled now, but her intention and meaning was perfectly clear to Jim. "I don't care about Romero, but I do care about those artifacts." She pulled once more on the ropes and stepped back.

Jim felt the pressure of his wrists lessen, and he shook the knots off. He worked his wrists and hands, trying to pump blood into them to get full use of them again.

"How did they get past you?" Margarita said, watching him wake up his wrists.

"I slept here last night, as a special precaution, and I heard the lock click. Romero opened the door and told me he was being taken as a hostage. The next thing I knew, a big guy with a scar on his head reached over Romero's shoulder and hit me on the head with a gun. Then I was out cold. When I woke up, I was tied and had a headache."

"It looks like they took most of the artifacts," she said. "Oh, Mr. Steel, can you really find them? This is such a big country, and they may have been gone for hours."

He was impressed by the expression on her face; she was so concerned. "They can't have gone too far too fast with a wagon, and they must have used one to move that much gold around. Yes, I'll catch up with them and recover your artifacts."

"I hope so," Margarita said, staring at the empty places on the shelves of the display.

Jim turned and ran outside into the early morning light. After looking for and finding the tracks, before normal traffic wiped them out, he went directly to the hotel where the rest of his men were staying. They had some gold to find.

"Let's rest here," Romero said in his thick accent. The man with the scar looked at him, then nodded. Good, Romero thought. It was far enough away, and besides, it was well after dawn. He hadn't planned to move this far from Sacramento, but he could always ride back.

The two wagons and ten men stopped around a huge old Colorado oak tree.

"Alright, men," Romero said. "This is far enough. I'll pay you, and then you can be getting back to Sacramento."

"Pay us in gold, you mean," one man said, a suspicious look on his face. "That's what you mean, ain't it?"

"Don't you mean we're going to divide up the gold now?" another said.

Romero looked around the men anxiously. "No," he said. "There seems to be a misunderstanding. I am paying you only for taking the gold this far. After that, I'll take care of it. I told you that in the first place," Romero said. He knew he was losing control of the men. The gold fever had struck them.

"Bullshit," one of the man said.

"Yeah, after all that work I done, I deserve one of the big statues," another said.

The man reached into the wagon. Seconds later, a slug slammed into the ground at the man's feet. He jerked his hand back and ran a few feet to the right.

"Nobody's taking nothing yet," the man with the scar said. He turned to Romero. "You never told us nothing about not splittin' up the gold," he said, eyeing Romero closely. "What're you tryin' to pull?"

Romero looked at the man worriedly. He didn't want to have a fight. He thought back carefully over what he had said to the men in the saloon last night. He had asked them to help him do a job; to get some gold. But he had never told them that they weren't sharing it!

"Well, I never told you we *were* sharing it," he said. "But I do have money here, plenty for everyone. Fifty dollars for every man."

"Chicken feed," one of them said.

"Yeah, I could've won that playing faro to-night. Let's get that gold!"

"Yeah! I've got a wife to feed!"

The men grew louder and more violent, while Romero and the scarred man watched them.

"Well, what's it going to be?" the disfigured man said to Romero.

Romero sweated. "But I can't let you take the gold," he said. His throat tightened, as he considered what might happen in the next few minutes. "Those are valuable museum pieces; works of art! It's not just gold, not just wealth . . . they're rare artifacts, far more valuable for what has been done with it, not what it is made of. Can't you see that?"

"I can see it glitter in the sun," one of the men said, and several others laughed.

"No! No!" Romero desperately looked from one man's face to another. "Can't you understand what I'm saying?"

"I understand enough," the man next to him said. "You're trying to cheat us, to keep all the gold for yourself."

Romero swallowed hard. The man stared at him. "It's not that at all," he said. "I'm not going to keep it. I'm going to give it back."

"What?" the men shouted.

"Well, I mean . . ." Romero was out of words. He could never explain his plan to them. It had worked so perfectly until now. He had stolen the gold pieces and would bring them back to Sacramento triumphantly. It would have been so perfect! And now these men were trying to keep him from carrying out his plan. He couldn't let them do it. He couldn't!

"Listen," he said. "Fifty dollars! That's a lot of money, more than most of you see in a month, right?" He remembered Jim Steel telling him that. "Just think of this as a night's work . . . for fifty dollars. That's fair, isn't it?"

"You make as much sense as a coyote preachin' a sermon," one man said. "I've had enough of this talk. When are we going to divide that gold?"

"Yeah," the man with the scar said. "We'll divide it up even like, but none of us is going back to Sacramento with it. Think about it. That gold's useless there for at least a few months. No one will touch it, and every lawman in town will be lookin' for it. It'll be dangerous to have it around."

"So?" one of the men asked.

"So, we take it into the hills, bury it, and save it for later, when everything settles down, and people forget about it."

The men grumbled among themselves.

"But we want it now!" one man said, echoing everyone's feelings.

"It ain't worth hen's teeth to you right now," he said. "So we'll all go out there, bury our shares somewhere in the hills, and then we can get it later and use it. And that way, no one'll know where the other man's is buried. That sounds good to me, don't it to you?"

The men nodded, but not happily.

"Good. Then let's go, before every lawman in Sacramento's after us."

"What about me?" Romero said, almost indignantly.

"What about you?" the scarred man said, and thought for a moment. "We'll leave you here, tied up to this tree. If anyone comes along, tell 'em what happened, and that they'll never find the gold, so they shouldn't even bother. It'll be scattered all over California by the time they get this far."

He took the cash from Romero's pocket, divided that up among the men, and then took a rope from his horse and tied Romero firmly to the tree. The rope bit into Romero's flesh as it was knotted for the last time.

"You won't get away with this," Romero said.

"I think we will. Alright, let's go!" the scarred man said, and the two wagons and ten men rode off, still heading south.

Alone at the tree, Romero cursed loud and long in Spanish. He had come so close to his deserved recognition. Now, because of greedy men, greedy Americans, his hopes were not only dashed, but he had lost, probably for all time, some of Mexico's greatest treasures. How could he live with himself after today?

Romero thought as he sat next to the tree, watching an ant crawl up the leg of his black pants. Jim Steel was surely smart enough to track the wagons and horses there. When he got there, what could Romero say?

He thought for a time, and finally came to a decision. Jim Steel would never recover the artifacts now; he'd also never find the men who stole them. So the best thing to do was to never mention his plan to Jim, about pretending to steal the gold.

There was no need now that the gold was really gone, and he really had been tied up by the men. They wouldn't be able to tell Jim otherwise, so why not just go along with the story that he had cooked up for Jim in the train car when they had unexpectedly met? There would be little he could add to the story, except that he had been left behind to tell Jim that he would never find the gold. . . .

Romero sighed. The rope cut into his stomach, making breathing painful. For the first time, he hoped he would see Jim Steel soon.

Minutes after Jim charged into the hotel, the army troopers were ready with their carbines and field rations. Horses were quickly hired for the men at a nearby livery stable, while Jim hired his own, a buckskin that looked a little like Hamlet, who was back in Denver. Jim wished he'd brought the horse with him, somehow, but he hadn't thought he'd be needing him on this trip again.

Jim brought his rifle and had packed his bags with rations before they picked up and started following the trail out of Sacramento. Studying the tracks, Jim saw that they had two wagons with them, and several horses; more than five or six, Jim was sure.

After a few miles, the tracks turned off the road and into the brush and rolling hillsides just outside of Sacramento. Time was important now. The longer they waited, the more chance of the gold being split up; if that happened, they would have to kiss it goodbye.

Jim wished he knew when the thieves had taken the gold, but he had nothing to go on. The guards they had found were still knocked out, and those who had been revived couldn't tell them when they had been attacked. Jim did know that it was dark, for he had seen Romero's face outlined by moonlight. That was the only clue he had. The thieves might have taken the gold six or seven hours ago, or more. If so, it would take longer to find them.

Sergeant Foster rode up alongside Jim.

"Sir?"

"Yeah?"

"How long do you think we'll be gone?"

Jim hesitated before answering. Each man packed three days rations, just in case. Water was easy to come by in the area, but all packed canteens as well, just in case.

"I don't know how long we'll be," Jim answered. "If it's much more than a day, I'll be surprised. They can't go fast with those wagons. We've got good men and we're bound to find them. Let's just hope that they didn't split up and go off in separate directions. That'll mean a lot more time."

"I don't understand," Foster said. "You said they can't go fast with wagons. Wouldn't they be going as fast as they could? Even wagons can manage pretty good speeds."

"That's true," Jim said. "But they are moving gold around, and gold's heavy. Slows you down every time. Besides, they might not want to damage any of the artifacts, though I doubt that would matter to them. They were probably just after the gold. But they also had a safe period of a least a few hours before anyone noticed that the gold was gone, with me out and their quiet work. These tracks don't show them running; no, not at all. It looks like they're walking their horses; see the clean hoofprint, and the short space between prints?" Jim said, pointing.

"Yeah," Sergeant Foster said. "But one thing still bothers me."

"What's that?" Jim asked, getting irritated by the man's talk.

"How do we know these are the right tracks?"

Jim looked at the man. "They are," he said. "They lead directly away from the area of the train car out of town. And they were the only ones that showed wagons."

"Granted," Foster said. "But how do you know that the gold isn't still in town somewhere? Hidden under a stack of petticoats, or in a trunk? We don't know for sure that it's even out of Sacramento yet. These tracks could have been made to fool us, or even made long before the robbery took place, and just happened to match what you think they should look like."

"No, I doubt it," Jim said, pointing to them as they rode along, the rest of the army troopers trailing behind them.

"See the tracks? The edges would be more crumbly, wetter if they'd been made early last night."

"How can you say that for sure?" Foster said, staring down at them, and then back up at Jim.

"It's the dew," Jim said. "From the looks of the tracks, they were made before the dewfall. If they had been made after dewfall, the ground would have been a touch wetter and the track wouldn't have been so clean."

"Really?" Foster said.

"Hell, I don't know," Jim answered. "It's just a theory of mine. But these are the right tracks; I'll bet on it."

Foster looked at Jim dubiously, then fell back. Jim was glad. He'd made up the story to get rid of the man, knowing how illogical it sounded. He didn't care. Sergeant Foster was a nice guy, but he got on Jim's nerves. And he didn't have time to talk now. He had to think, hard and fast.

Chapter Eleven

Jim brought his horse to a stop. He'd just topped a small hill and had a panoramic view of the surrounding countryside. It was covered with ancient trees: maples, laurels, Douglas firs, and was crisscrossed with rivers; a vibrant, alive land that now held a mystery for Jim Steel.

Where had the tracks gone?

They had been following them for hours. It was now after three in the afternoon, and suddenly there was no trail. Not a trace. Jim frowned. On this high rock, the wagons hadn't left a clean trail, and there was no brush to mark the passage, no dust on the rock to show hoofprints — nothing

"We'll stop here and give the horses a blow," Jim said. "I'm going to ride on ahead to see if I can pick up their trail again. This rock didn't leave anything to follow, but I'm sure I'll pick up their tracks again not far. I hear water ahead and they may have stopped. There'll be prints around it."

"Right," Foster said.

Jim rode out slowly, letting the horse walk free. He scanned the ground on each side for several feet as they moved along. Minutes later there were still no tracks or clues that anybody had been there in a long time. Finally, Jim moved down into a forested area and quickly found where the brush had been broken back by the big wagons. He followed the markings for a few yards until the sound of splashing grew louder. Jim headed for it, to give his horse a drink.

After riding past a thicket of madrone and elder, he found it. It was a graceful waterfall, curving out from the lip of a hill, arching majestically in the late afternoon sun, and plunging into a deep, cool blue pool at its base. Jim rode up and let the buckskin drink deeply of the water as he studied the ground. Tracks all over.

Jim got off his horse and took a drink, then mounted and rode along the tracks fifty yards, until he was sure that they not only were the right ones, but that they wouldn't stop again soon after they started. They didn't, so Jim rode back to meet with his other men, who stood waiting.

"Found a good set of tracks," he said to Sergeant Foster. "Follow me."

The ride there was silent. Jim could have kicked himself remembering how the man with the scar on his face had knocked him out before he did anything. If he had acted quickly, he wouldn't be in this mess. He had been listening to Romero's story so intently that he didn't even see the gun butt, until it was coming down on his head. It would never happen again, he told himself, feeling the spot. It was still sore, alright, and the hurt made him even more intent on finding the gold artifacts.

Foster took his men to the waterfall, where all drank, filled their canteens, and watered their horses. Afterward, they were quickly off again on the new trail.

They followed it, increasing speed, urgent to find the men. It was still early in the afternoon, and Jim was fairly confident that they'd find the men before sundown. He hoped so, at any rate, for he didn't want to spend another night away from the gold.

Something up ahead made Jim's eyes flicker back to it. It looked out of place. He gazed at it and saw what it was; a red-and-white checkered piece of cloth. It hung down from an oak tree, close to the ground.

Jim held up his hand in a silent command for all men to stop their horses. He got off his, and walked carefully toward the tree. What was it?

Jim stalked the tree, taking no chances, crouching behind rocks and other trees as he moved. Finally, he worked his way around the other side, and had a clear view of the tree. Jim lifted his head out from behind a bush and stared at the scene.

Rafael Romero, the director of the Mexico City Museum of Culture, sat, his head slumped to his chest, tied to a tree.

Jim ran up and slapped the man's face. Yes, he was still alive; the head rolled and the eyes opened. Finally, the voice came, groggy, but there.

"What? Where? Oh, it is you, Jim Steel," Romero said. He licked his chapped lips and seemed to have difficulty swallowing. "Thank

God you have come. I thought I would die tied to this tree."

Jim bent and loosened the knots.

"They did this to you?"

Romero nodded. "They decided they'd had enough of me, and that I couldn't do any harm. Oh," Romero said, fully waking up. "They also told me to tell you not to bother following them."

"What did they mean by that?" Jim asked, pulling one end of the knot through a loop, loosening it.

"They said that they were going to split up the gold in equal shares for all the men, then each man was going to bury his share somewhere up in the hills," Romero said. "Each one's burying his own; that way, no one knows where more than one cache is."

Jim frowned. "They're not going to melt it down?" he asked, thinking that would be the first thing they'd do.

"No," Romero said. "They decided it would be too dangerous to bring it back into town." Romero coughed. "They'll wait and do that later, when everyone's forgotten about it, and each man'll bring his own. That way they'll be safe, they think. Can I have a drink, Mr. Steel? My throat is so dry from the sun," he said, as Jim finally got the knots out, and pulled the rope off the man's hands.

Jim handed Romero the canteen and watched him drink. Romero's face was burned slightly by the sun, his lips were dry and cracked, and his wrists were white. Judging from the looks of him, he'd been there three or four hours, four at the most. The robbers were still far ahead of them. They hadn't been riding fast or hard enough. Well, Jim thought, after he took care of Romero, he'd ride twice as hard.

But that was another problem, he realized, as he thought of it. What could he do with Romero? He didn't have a horse for the man, and he wasn't in any condition to go with them.

Jim thought for a moment, as Romero wiped water from his lips, and sighed after swallowing. The only solution was to find a man who was willing to take Romero back to Sacramento. He was sure there was at least one man who wouldn't mind giving up the search. Jim knew it from experience.

Jim took the canteen from Romero, and slung it back on his saddle.

"Can you tell me how long ago they left you here?" Jim asked Romero.

He shook his head. "No. It was a long time ago; at least, my sores tell me it was so. I fell asleep," he said. "But it might have been a few hours before noon. Yes, that would probably be about right. I remember the way the light slanted through the trees."

Jim nodded. "Well, you want to go back to town, or come with us?" Jim asked. "There's no other choice."

Romero looked at Jim, and then to the ground. "I should go with you and get the artifacts back," he said, softly, "but I fear that you will come home empty-handed. I don't see how you can possibly find them, when they're probably dug into half the countryside by now. I'm sure the men didn't go much further from where we are now to their hiding."

"Maybe," Jim said. "But maybe not. There's another thing I need to ask. Had they divided up the pieces by the time they left? Or left you?"

"No, they hadn't," Romero said. "But what does that have to do with anything?"

"Well, if I know this type of men, they'll be a long argument about who gets what, and at least one man will get trigger-happy. That discussion in itself could take an hour or more. No, we're not too late, but we've got to move fast. And first, I've got to take care of you. So what'll it be, Romero? Will you come along with us, or go back to town? You have to share a horse either way, and it doesn't matter to me what you do. But we haven't much time. We've got to leave now and cover as much distance as possible. I want to catch them before tonight. So how about it?" he asked Romero, who still sat leaning against the tree.

Romero thought, hard. He was in a situation. He thought that Jim Steel had a chance to get the gold now, if what he said about the fight that the men could have about the gold was true. If so, he'd like to be there and play some part in recovering it. But if any of the thieves survived and talked, who would Jim Steel believe — him, or the thief? Romero didn't know, and he didn't think he could take the chance.

Jim was waiting for his answer. He'd have to make up his mind fast. He wanted to say yes, he'd go along with them, but knew he was too afraid of what the robbers would say. He could deny it, of course, but when faced with the robbers and Jim Steel at the same time, Romero didn't think he could take it. He looked up at Jim.

"I don't feel like riding," he said weakly.

"You have to," Jim said. "Or we'll just leave you here."

Romero decided. "Alright," he said, standing up. "I will go back to Sacramento."

Satisfied with the man's answer, Jim whistled, and called the army troopers from where they had been waiting.

"Do I have a volunteer to take Romero back to town, and to relay a message to Margarita Contreras?"

The closest man to Jim stepped forward. "Yes, sir," he said.

"Good," Jim said. "Romero'll have to ride double with you, since he doesn't have a horse of his own."

"I understand," the young man in blue said, mounting and then glancing at Romero, who stood in front of the tree, his knees shaky.

"Can you find your way back to Sacramento?" Jim asked the man.

"Yes, sir, I can."

"Good." Jim helped Romero up onto the horse. The man grabbed wildly as he nearly fell off. His hand finally grasped the young soldier's belt. Jim steadied Romero, and when he was sure that he was set, he spoke again.

"Rest up at the hotel," he said to Romero. Then, turning to the soldier, he said, "Tell Miss Contreras everything that has happened so far, and that we are on the trail, and hope to have the thieves caught soon."

The man nodded and rode off.

One problem out of his life, Jim thought, as he watched them go. He then turned to his men.

"Listen up," he said. "We'll go on again. There ain't no chance trying to track at night, so we'll have to find them before dusk if it's to be today. Even if we don't, the thieves have to stop and rest, for they're sure not crazy enough to bury gold at night. There's too good a chance that they'd never find the place again after it got light. So it should be safe for us to stop if we have to, but let's not have to," Jim said.

"If we spend the night," he continued, "we'll strike out at dawn again. If any of you see anything at anytime that looks suspicious, tell me or your sergeant. If you don't think you should shout it out, then come up and tell us direct." Jim repeated all the instructions he had given them earlier that morning before they rode out.

They followed the trail through the trees, and past vistas overlooking masses of untouched wilderness. Several times, the trail followed the course of streams at which, Jim could tell from the tracks, the men had stopped for water. Once they too stopped, watering their horses and filling their canteens. Afterwards, Jim pressed the men on, telling them to keep quiet. He had a feeling.

But half an hour later, they still had no sign of them. The tracks continued on, two wagons and several horses. At least they hadn't split up. Jim hoped he could find them before those wagons — or the gold — went their separate ways.

The men stood around the wagon, looking over the gold pieces. One young man pointed out a nude figure of a woman, primitively done, but defined enough to be popular among the men.

"I get the golden girl," he said, reaching for it.

"Like hell!" another said.

"I decide who gets what," a voice said from behind them.

The men turned to look. It was the man with the scar over his eye. He stood near the wagon staring at them.

"Yeah? Well, who picked you? I don't owe you anything. Why can't I decide? Why can't we all decide?"

The men around him backed his questions with shouts of "right" and "good", but the scar-faced man shook his head.

"No," he said. "I'll decide. If you do it, it'll take all day. It's good gold, and we can all tell whether a piece weighs more than another. Sure, it's not going to be exact, but this ain't exactly Wesley's Assay Office."

A few of the men laughed; the young man who had argued felt that he had lost some support.

"No, wait!" he said. "Shouldn't we decide this thing fairly?"

"There ain't no fair out here, boy," the man said. There were fifteen years and a hell of a lot of experience between the two. "There's only what you can make out of the spot you've got yourself in. Well, we got ourselves into this one, and we'll get ourselves out."

"You'll get yourself out," the man said accusingly. "You just want to get most of the gold for yourself."

"You've been out in the sun too long, boy," the scarfaced man said. "You ain't talkin' right. So why don't you just sit your ass down, and shut your mouth. We've got more important things to do."

The young man's hand went to his holster. At that instant, the older man swung around, drew, and blasted a slug that tore the button off the kid's shirt sleeve.

"I said, sit down," he repeated to the stunned youth.

He nodded and did so, cursing under his breath.

The scarred man looked at the two wagons full of gold, and at the nine other men. It would be a messy business dividin' up all that, but it had to be done. And soon. They had four or five hours before sundown, and it would be good if they could get it over with by then. Grouped up together like they were, they were just askin' for trouble. He had no doubt that there were men out looking for them. They didn't have time to listen to some kid cryin' about a piece he fancied.

He walked back to the wagon and looked at the gold. It gleamed in the sunlight, waiting. Waiting to be taken. But the hardest part was ahead. How in the hell could he control gold-fevered men? He knew they'd never agree to the way he divided up the gold, 'cause they all had their own way of doing it. Well, he'd just have to back up himself with his Colt .45. It had come in handy in the past, and he'd probably need to use it again today. He'd get that gold laid out and then be done with the thing. He'd make sure he got his fair share, of course, but knew it would be a risk to take that little extra that he wanted. He might try it anyway, just to show the other men who the hell was boss around here.

"Alright, men," he said. "We'll do this thing fairly. I don't want to cheat any of you. If you think you're getting less than the others, tell me; but don't go drawing, or you'll not be needing any gold where you'll be going. We have to do this thing right quick and get the hell out of here, before Sacramento comes lookin' for us."

The men nodded in agreement; they were eager. A few of them looked over their shoulders, as if to make sure that no one was watching them.

The scarfaced man was ready to call the men

to come up so he could start dividing, when the younger man who had argued with him suddenly jumped to his feet and dashed for the nearest wagon. He hopped up on the seat and slapped the reins. The tired horses responded, just as there was a gunshot, and the boy slumped down on the seat, a slug through his heart. The horses, startled by the noise, stamped and neighed, then started to run, taking the gold with them.

Several men hurried up to them and got the beasts calmed down before they got far away. By this time, the scarred man had slipped his gun back into his holster and stood looking at the rest of the men.

"That just means more for the rest of us," he said. "But don't go tryin' it, or all you'll get is a plot of ground without any Bible verses."

The men looked at each other, as if in silent agreement not to do anything as wild as the boy had. They were impatient, the man with scar could see. Good. Maybe they wouldn't be so sensitive when he started passing out the gold.

"Hey, I'm hungry," one man said.

"Did you bring any food?"

"Sure, didn't you?"

Soon all the men were talking about the food they did or didn't bring; the apple pie Betty had baked that morning that waited at home for them; the hardtack and salt pork they had packed in their saddlebags. They made so much noise about food and eating — and the scarred man realized that they hadn't done that for over twelve hours — that he decided it would be a good idea to eat then.

"Alright," he said. "Those of you who brought food, we'll break to eat. Hell, I'm hungry, too. And we'll need that food to get the gold buried after it's divided even. So eat, and after that, it's the gold." He appointed a guard — a man who had not brought any food along with him — to keep watch in the woods to make sure no one came up on them while they ate. It was getting later in the day, and he could feel trouble coming.

The men made their meals, such as they had. One man lit a fire in the center of the clearing, and another who had planned well brought out a can of peaches, which he devoured with obvious relish.

Other men, who hadn't brought food, rolled cigarettes and watched the smoke drift up into the air. For the moment, the gold was forgotten; after all, what good was it if they couldn't use it?

The scarfaced man smiled as he smoked and watched the men eat. It would give him more time to figure out just how the hell he could divide the gold up without getting killed doing it.

Chapter Twelve

Jim stopped his buckskin on a small rise and turned his head to the west. Raising his hand to signal the ten mounted men behind him to stop and be quiet, he listened closely. What had he heard? For a moment, it had sounded like a signal gunshot, and Jim had hoped there would be more. Now all he heard was the wind. Whatever had happened, it was over now.

Jim and his men continued. They jogged along easily most places, following the wide tracks of the wagon. It was almost impossible to hide the route of the two heavy wagons, as they plowed through the fields and foothills. Now they followed them alongside a stream. Steel wondered how far in they would go to hide the gold.

Jim had hoped that the shot might be a sign of trouble among the robbers; an argument, a fight, or something that would slow them down.

His mounted troopers should overtake the wagons soon now. The lumbering, heavily laden wagons couldn't make good time. But the compact fighting unit he had could move quickly. If all went right, they should be able to ambush the robbers and cut them down, before they knew they were being followed.

The trail led past a stand of cottonwoods, and around a bend where the stream entered much thicker timber, and Steel wondered how the wagons would get through. Jim smelled something. He sniffed the air and held up his hand to signal the men to stop. It was smoke. Someone had lit a fire.

Jim tied his buckskin to a sapling, then darted ahead to a pine and peered around it. Not yet. He moved in short dashes between cover and concealment, following the scent of smoke as he went. The wind blew steadily towards him, so he could be fairly sure of the direction.

After about a quarter of a mile, he saw that the heavy timber slanted off to the left and up a ravine, while the stream continued on straight ahead, into a small meadow where trees grew at the water's edge.

He looked around the sturdy trunk of an oak, and ahead he saw a lone man, sitting by the stream, smoking. He was fifty yards away, with his back to Jim. Jim moved like a shadow from tree to tree, moving closer to the man.

The man must be a rear guard, he guessed. The smoke smell was much stronger now; they must be near the robber's campsite. Jim spurted ahead again, and now was within thirty feet of the man. He drew his six-inch hunting knife and edged closer. When he was twenty feet away from the man, he balanced the knife, gripped it by the back of the blade, and threw it.

There was a soft sound like stepping in mud when the knife drove into the rear guard's back. He fell forward, facedown, in the stream, without a cry.

Steel ran forward, stepped into the stream, and pulled the body out, using the man's wet hair. He rolled it over and studied the face. He couldn't remember seeing it before. When Jim got back to the edge of the small clearing, he saw Sergeant Foster approaching with his men. Foster waved his troops up and came ahead with Jim's horse.

"They're close," Jim said. "They had out a rear guard. When we find them, we'll try to get them in crossfire. You lead my horse and keep me in sight. Let's move with no sound at all."

Jim ran ahead and the troopers followed, spread out, yet in contact. Jim continued to follow his nose; the fragrant smoke grew stronger. In a minute, he heard voices, and finally he saw them.

The two wagons were in a small clearing, flooded with sunlight, the men gathered around the fire. They were eating and smoking. The horses were tied up at the far end, and one of the wagons was uncovered. Where the sun struck the gold, it was blinding.

Jim worked his way closer, never making a sound, until he could hear what the men were talking about.

A tall man with a scar sat off from the others, smoking. A thinner man walked up to him.

"When we gonna' start dividin' up the gold?" he asked.

"When everybody's done," the man with the scar said. "Won't be long."

"Ain't you worried about the law?"

"We got a guard; he'll tell us if he sees anything."

Jim edged away from the pine tree he had been behind and worked his way silently back toward Foster and his men. The sergeant was a hundred yards away.

"How many?" he asked.

"Eight or nine," Jim said. "A big one with a scar on his face seems to be the leader. Looks like they're gettin' ready to split up the gold. We got here just in time." He spoke in a whisper. "You stay here, then in fifteen minutes, move up and get into position. Give every man a target, a specific man to shoot. I'll move around as far to the other side as I can, without getting into your line of fire. Be ready, and when I fire, then have your men fire. We should be able to get half of them on the first volley. Be sure they use their carbines."

Foster nodded. Jim took the first five men, after they'd tied their mounts up, and worked them silently away from the stream into the side of the slope a hundred yards from the water. They crept forward until they were past the smell of the smoke, and worked back down the slope. Steel could just see the encampment, and the men sitting around the fire. A few of them got up and started milling around the wagons, looking over the gold.

Another three or four minutes, and they all would be in position. Jim checked his watch. They were overdue.

Suddenly, he heard a shout from somewhere below him. A gunshot sounded from downstream. Every man in the camp grabbed a gun.

"Ambush! Ambush!" a man said, running through the trees and bursting out into the camp.

Almost at once, six army rifles cracked below. But already, men had jumped onto each wagon and began moving them out of the camp. The other men mounted, and they all urged the wagons forward.

Steel and his men were partly shielded by the brush. They ran ahead, then flopped down on the ground and began firing through a screening of brush at the departing robbers. The driver on the last wagon turned to look behind him, and a rifle bullet drilled through his chest. He fell forward, the lines wrapping around his body and pulling tight on the horses. It tugged them to a stop. One of the robbers looked back, tried to spur the horses forward, but a rain of bullets slapped around him and he darted forward, spurring his mount on at a full gallop.

Jim and his men ran into the cleared section, but all the men had left. The one gold wagon rested where the horses had stopped it, and Jim ran to it, rolled the driver onto the ground, and drove the wagon into the trees to hide it.

Sergeant Foster ran into the clearing, swearing at everything. He checked the two bodies on the ground, one of the driver and another one near the trampled fire. He came up to Steel and saluted.

"Sir, report two casualties on the enemy side. We had one man slightly nicked by a pistol round. Near as I can figure, a man was going to relieve the rear guard. Well, he walked right in on us, took a shot, and ran like hell back to camp. Must've seen our uniforms," Foster said.

Jim thanked the sergeant and had him bring up the horses.

"We'll leave three men here to guard the wagon, and push on ahead after the other one. Romero said they had ten men, and we've accounted for three of them, so they're down to seven. Now we have them outnumbered. Get the men ready just as soon as you can. Stay back a good fifty yards from me. We don't want to bump into another rear guard like that one."

The trail of the wagon and the fleeing men was easy to follow, and the bandits knew that they could not move as fast as their pursuers. Jim expected delaying actions, and the first wasn't long in coming. They had positioned two men behind rocks ahead where the valley narrowed. The trail went between the two rocks. Jim felt the impact of the bullet before he heard the sound of the rifle. The slug hit a pine tree he was standing beside and splattered bark into his face. He rolled backwards, down a slight incline, glad that he had decided to check the spot out on foot first.

Jim waved up Sergeant Foster, who sent two men on foot through the timber to the left to outflank. By the time the soldiers got in position to fire on the roadblock, the robbers had moved on. The two men waved Jim on, then hurried back to their mounts as Jim probed forward.

The wagon tracks of the heavily loaded vehicle stretched out across a small valley which was waist deep in soft summer grass that had matured and was silky brown and dry as tinder. On the other side of the valley, about a quarter of a mile ahead, lay a small pass, and Jim could see the wagon tracks showing plainly on it.

Jim and the troopers gathered together at the edge of the valley. They would ride across in a group, and then scatter, making themselves less of a target than if they went across one at a time. That way, they could be picked off by a good rifleman.

They were nearly halfway across the valley with a strong wind blowing toward them, when Jim smelled smoke again. Then, directly in front of them, they saw a billow of smoke, then flames. Grass fire! It was a phrase of terror on the plains, and just as much of one there in that small valley. It blew straight toward them, and now Jim saw flames curling around on either side of them. They were trapped! They couldn't outrace the fire to the rear, and they couldn't go forward, or to either side.

Jim leaped off his horse, and looked at the raging fire coming at them less than a hundred yards away. He broke off matches from a packet of stinkers and began setting the grass at his feet on fire. The fire raced away with them in the wind. The men quickly got the idea, and lit a swath of grass twenty yards wide and watched it burn to the rear, the wind carrying it. The grass burned off quickly and died into smoking blackness. As soon as the flames were out, Jim and the army men moved onto the charred ground, and watched as the wall of flames that raced toward them met the edge of the blackened spot, and died out for lack of fuel.

The men looked at Jim and gave him silent thanks.

"Mount up," he said. "We've got to make up some lost time now."

There was no reception party waiting for them at the pass. The watchers could see nothing for the smoke from the front of the fire, since it all blew backwards with the flames. From the front, it could have looked like the troopers and Jim were all burned up in the flames.

Jim didn't let them ride through the pass. He stopped and crawled on the ground with Foster until they could see over it. Lying on their bellies, they discussed the view. The wagon track disappeared in the distance, and smoke from the fire hung in the air, further obscuring the view.

Jim wished he had the binoculars he had used in the war. Down the valley somewhere, there was a wagon and six or seven riders, and he couldn't see one of them. He cupped his hands around his eyes to concentrate his vision, squinted down a little, and then he could make it out.

"There's something," he said to Foster. "About three miles down, there's a ranch of some kind."

"A ranch?" Foster said.

"Yeah. Wonder if our boys stopped in there."

"Mighty likely," Foster agreed.

They pushed their way back down the incline so that they could sit up without being seen, then moved back to their mounts, and rode alongside the ridge until they came to the wooded part, where they could go over the ridge without being seen, in case the thieves had used a spotter.

They rode hard through the woods, down over a small hog-back, then down a long finger valley that would come out into the main flatness ahead. When they were still a little above the valley floor, Jim checked their location.

"We swing back to the north just a hair, and we'll be right in line with the ranch we saw. Only one in the whole valley I could see, so I'd give you dollars to doughnuts that's where they're headed." Jim checked the sun. "Too early to charge in there for supper with them. Nowhere near to dark. Let's move up as close as we can, and then I'll go in there and reconnoiter the place."

They followed the ridge line until it gave way to the south, then crossed over a low lying valley and one more ridge, before they could see the buildings ahead. It seemed to be more farm than ranch, with plowed fields surrounding the house, and a large barn. A dozen head of beef roamed one fenced pasture, and beyond they saw some sheep. They sat on their mounts in the splash of trees about a quarter of a mile from the buildings.

"Smoke coming out of the chimney," Foster said.

"There comes a rider in from the northwest. That's where we were. He's probably saying we fried in that bonfire they set for us," Jim said, watching the man move.

"Well, Captain, what do we do?" Foster asked.

"I go in as a fiddle-footed range hand looking for work. That way we find out who is there and what's going on."

"But won't they recognize you from the train? You said that one big guy, the one with the scar, knocked you out."

"I think he did see me, but it was dark inside the car, and he couldn't have gotten a very good look. I'll put on a heavy accent and confuse him," Jim said.

"Might be better, sir," Foster said, "if we moved up there and did a soft recon, just looked over the place with two or three men in the weeds outside."

"You'd play hell getting close enough to see anything in your blue pants and shirts. They know the troopers are after them. At least I'll have a chance. You hear any shooting, you come storming with your rifles at the ready and order everyone outside."

Sergeant Foster frowned. He'd grown to admire this tough, ex-officer who seemed to know exactly what he was doing. Now he was sure the man had seen a lot of battle experience during the war.

"Yes, sir. If that's what you think is best. I'll try to get some men on each side, as close as we can without giving away our positions."

"All I can ask," Jim said, checking his gear.

He decided to ride downstream a mile or so, find a road or trail that must lead in toward Sacramento, and come up the trail, rather than overland. That would be another plus, if the robbers really were there.

With a wave, he rode off, telling the troopers to have a cold meal while he was gone.

It took him the better part of an hour to go below the ranch, find the lane that led into the buildings, and then ride up it at a walk, unhurried, the way a grub-line rider usually does. He's got his next meal in sight, and there's no rush now. Almost any ranch, cabin, or farm in the West gives a lonely rider a meal and heads him out for the next ranch. Unless the ranch has been taken over by robbers and killers.

Jim heard nothing unusual as he rode up toward the place, but none of the normal activities of a farm or ranch were going on around the buildings — nobody feeding stock, chopping wood, drawing water at the well. He sat a minute at the hitching rail outside the ranch house, then got down wearily, wrapped the reins around the pole, and stretched as if he'd been in the saddle for a long time. He pushed his hat back on his head, adjusted it a little lower, and walked slowly towards the ranch-house door.

It opened before he got there. A man came out, a pistol in his holster, and a frown on his face.

"Yeah, you want something, stranger?"

"Well, howdy there. Just wonderin' if you needed any hands? Got myself some spare time, and I'm lookin' for some work. Do range work and ranchin' did a little farming once up in Oregon."

The man at the door hooked his thumbs in his belt and snorted. "I'll be damned, you still using that old one? You're a grub-stake rider, pure and simple. Seen hundreds of you bums. Don't know why we put up with you no-goods. Never done a lick of work in your life. You better just mount up and ride on. We got no spare grub around here for you."

Jim chuckled. "Yes, sir. I done heared that before, too. Fact is, I chop a mean pile of cord-wood. I pitch hay like tarnation, and I even clean out stables. Work for my grub, deed I do. Don't make no cash money, but I work lots."

"Well, you can just work somewhere else. Git moving."

The door pushed wider, and another man stepped out. He was the tall one with a scar on his face, the one Jim had seen starting to divide up the gold.

"Well now, maybe you're being too hard on the gent. Where you say you was from?"

"All the same to you, I didn't say," Jim answered.

"Yeah, figgers. I've been in the same situation." The big man stared at him a minute. "Just wondered, thought for a minute there I might know you from Texas."

"Don't reckon. I'm working west from Kansas, Dodge City."

"Uh, huh. Come on in now and have a bite. We got plenty," the man with the scar said, with a smile.

The other man shrugged and went back inside. The door gaped open invitingly.

"Well, tarnation. A body sure could stand some victuals, if'n you was so inclined." Jim stepped into the ranch house, and turned as the big man came in behind him. The first man who had talked to him stood to one side, holding a shotgun aimed at Jim's stomach. Both hammers were cocked.

The man with the scar lost his smile.

"Now, mister, you tell us just who the hell you are, or you got about twenty seconds to live."

Chapter Thirteen

Jim Steel stared into the twin black holes of death, and then looked up at the big man with the scar.

"Like I say, I'm on the grub-line, don't tend to stay in one place too long."

"Lies!" the smaller man said. "That buckskin you got is a long-winded critter. Any grubstake rider would've sold him for beans and board long before now. So who are you?"

"Down on my luck, that's who. Not lookin' for trouble. Hell, no reason for the scatter gun. You don't want me here, I'll ride out. Most folks hereabouts are a mite bit more friendly."

"We're not." The men talked together in whispers for a minute.

"Okay, okay!" the smaller one said. "I'd just as soon blow his head off. I don't like the looks of him."

The larger man moved behind Jim and slid the .45 out of his holster, checked the cylinders and then pushed it into his own belt.

"Come on. Out to the barn. You give me just one small excuse, and I'll blow you in half, you hear me?"

"I hear. I ain't lookin' for trouble."

Jim walked to the barn, thirty yards across the yard from the house. The man told Jim to unlatch the bar that was across the big door leading into the barn. Steel did, then found himself pushed inside. Seconds later, the barn door slammed shut and he heard the bar drop into place.

It was almost dark inside the big barn. He could tell he was in a part that had a double storey on it, and he felt that there were others there.

"Hello, anyone there? Look, I'm not here to hurt anyone. Are there other people in here being held prisoner?"

A small "yes" came from the area ahead of him. Jim still had his matches, but didn't want to risk striking one. Not yet. He found his eyes adjusting to the dim light in the barn, and he saw ahead of him an elderly man and woman in chairs by a small table.

Steel went up to them and saw that they were in their sixties, worked-worn and used up, clinging to life, because it was the best option they had left.

"Are you one of them?" the little woman asked. She wore a sunbonnet, and a faded print dress. Her hands and arms were thin, with skin bunched and loose over the bones and tendons.

"No, I'm not one of them," Jim said. "I'm a prisoner like you. How many of them are there?"

"Six," the man said, his voice strangely firm. "Six, and they came in shooting this afternoon. Killed my foreman and one hand, run off two others. Said they're going to live here from now on. We can't get away to ask for help."

"Did they bring a wagon?"

"Wagon?" the man asked. He nodded. "Yes,

they had a wagon, loaded heavy, but had a cover over it, blanket of some kind."

"Where did they put it?"

"Over there," he said. "You walked right by it."

Jim looked back, saw the wagon, and ran to it. It was the one, filled to the gills with the gold artifacts. He went back to the old couple.

"Those men are robbers and killers," he said. "I've been tracking them, and now we have them. I have help outside. Is there any way out of here?"

"They locked all the doors from the outside. Nailed two windows shut and one door. Can't get out, they told us."

"Is there a haymow?"

" 'Course, sonny, this is a barn."

"Is the mow door open?"

"Yep, middle of the season. What tomfoolery kind of question is that?"

Jim saw the ladder that went up to the half hayloft. He climbed it and looked at the splash of light that came through the mow door. The door opened away from the house, and it was set up for haying. The big fork on a long rope hung in the middle of the loft, and a cable stretched to the ground at a 45-degree angle. It came from the very top of the mow, where a track could be used to push the big fork back to the loft section. Jim saw the ladder built up the stud wall on the face of the barn that went all the way to the peak of the roof, for servicing the track or unsnarling the ropes and cables. He hurried down to the old farmer.

"Do you have any axle grease around here?"

"What's a farm, sonny, without a can or two of axle grease?" He laughed. "Tarnation, sonny, 'course we got axle grease. Right over there under that tarp is my workbench. Haven't used it much lately, though."

Jim ran to the tarp and pulled it back. He found the axle grease, and something else he could use, a three-foot-long piece of half-inch cable. He put it in the bench vice and bent it in the middle, then he bent up a 90-degree angle on each end. He lathered the end of the long U-shaped bend with axle grease, and told the old people to stay right where they were. He would be back with help, but they shouldn't tell the thieves that.

"I look like a loony, sonny? 'Course we won't tell them."

Carrying the bent cable, Jim climbed the ladder to the loft, then went up the boards nailed to the studs that formed a crude ladder to the very top of the barn. He reached out and slipped the bent steel cable over the other cable and saw that it would slide easy. He knew he would slide fast, and perhaps hit hard, but it was better than jumping out the fourteen-foot long barn door to the ground below.

He saw a man come out of the ranchhouse and walk to the outhouse just up from the barn. The man vanished inside for a moment. When he came back, he started for the barn, changed his mind, and went back into the house. When the house door slammed, and Jim couldn't see anyone, he caught the bent up ends of the cable, gripped them carefully, and then let his weight sag on the cable. His bent cable holder slid away from him. He held with his feet for a moment, then let go, and immediately slid down the cable with surprising speed. As he neared the ground, he held his feet in front of him and decided he would roll to the left, away from the post buried in the ground that held the cable.

He hit the ground with his feet, let go of the cable, skewed sideways, and rolled over four times in the farmyard dirt. Then he was on his feet, running away from the house and barn toward the small grove of trees to the west. He hoped that was where he'd left Sergeant Foster and his men.

"Mr. Steel, you've found us," Foster said. They talked it over for fifteen minutes.

"The problem is to get them out of the house," Jim said. "I won't turn that old couple's home into a battleground. We get them outside, or wait until they come out. The wagon of gold is in the barn. They'll probably make a break for it tonight, when it gets dark."

For another five minutes, they planned how they would handle it. At last they had it. There were three doors to the ranch house, and no other bunkhouses. The men must all be in the one house. They would put one man covering each door. The moment a robber came out of the house, he would be shot. They might pick off one or two that way, then the rest would make a break for the barn and try to get away with the wagon.

"They have to try for the wagon," Jim said. "It's all of their chips in the game. Without that, they come away with nothing."

"The old folks are in the barn?" Foster asked.

"Yes, but we can fire across the doorway without putting them in danger. Or we can let the robbers get the wagon out in the open, and then charge them."

"I know the best way," Foster said. "I know it's not good soldiering, or good western horsethinking, but we could let them hitch up and get the wagon out of the barn. Then, when they are in the middle of the road, we shoot the lead horse. Put it down, and stop the wagon, then pick off the bandits who are still alive."

Steel thought about it. At last, he nodded. "I don't like killing a horse either, but it's a sight better than putting that old couple in danger. People come before horses."

Foster faded into the cornstalks to talk to his men. They had their instructions, and soon the riflemen were positioned within a hundred yards of the three doors on the ranch house. Sergeant Foster and Jim and three more troopers were covering the front door of the barn.

"Why don't we throw a scare into them right now?" Jim said. "They know the cavalry is after them — they saw you. Why don't we put one of your troopers on a horse, run him in to about five hundred yards of the place, and blast a couple of pistol shots at the house, and then haul ass out of there? We might draw one or two of them out in the open where we could cut them down."

"I couldn't ask a trooper to do that," Foster said. "They've got one rifle, and probably stole another one in that ranch. It's too dangerous."

He got up in the cornstalk cover and moved to the rear. Jim followed him. "Hey, where are you going?"

Foster laughed. "To play bait, but my horse is a quarter of a mile back there in those trees."

Jim laughed and let him go. He had the sergeant's rifle and zeroed it on the front door of the ranch house. He had given strict instructions not to fire into the windows or doors of the house.

Fifteen minutes later, and well before dark, Sergeant Foster rode hard across a wheat field toward the front of the house, wheeled at the near fence, and fired two shots at the house that fell far short. The front screen banged and a man ran out with a rifle. Before he could get a shot off, two rifles from the far side of the buildings fired. The man spun, hit by both bullets, and went down. He tried to crawl back to the ranch-house, but a moment later, he gave up and his hand stretched out.

One down, thought Jim. Six to go. Or was it five? The old man had told him that six men, not seven, were there.

Foster rode out of rifle range quickly, circling far to the south, away from the position of any of the troops. He was back in the cornfield a half hour later and saw the effect of his work.

"Now all we have to do is wait until it gets dark and they make their play," Jim said.

He shared the cold field rations of hardtack and salt pork, and washed it down with water. A rifle shot racked behind the house, and then all was silent until dusk settled in.

Jim went over the plans again with Sergeant Foster. "We want them to come out the front door. It's closer to the barn door," Jim said. "So get word to your men on the front door to let the robbers come out that way. I hope the horses are in the barn. I never did check that out."

Foster sent a runner to tell the man covering the front door about the new instructions. He also ordered the men to move up to twenty-five yards as soon as it was fully dark. At twenty-five yards, they could see the doors plainly.

Nothing happened for an hour. Jim and his team moved up, too, until they were less than thirty yards from the barn, lying in a ditch that was now dry and filled with grass.

An hour after dark, a rifle in back of the house spoke, then again and again. Several pistol shots returned the fire, and Jim hoped that the riflemen had good cover.

They heard the spring on the front screen-door squeak, as the door opened. A shadow darted out, then another, and both ran to the barn. No shots came. Two more men left the house and ran to the barn.

"Let them come," Jim whispered. The last man left the house then, and the barn door moved. Jim saw the big door open, and the men pushed the wagon half out the door. Almost at the same time, a man came around from the back of the barn with four horses, already harnessed. They hadn't been harnessed that quickly; they must have been ready to go. The men waited, as they watched the robbers hitch up to the tongue and the double trees on the wagon. Then three men climbed on board, and two more mounted horses, and they cracked reins and the wagon moved down the lane. Jim, Foster, and the three troopers paralleled the lane, running along in the cornfield. When they were a hundred yards from the buildings, Jim said one word.

"Now!"

The running men stopped, took aim, and fired. Each had been assigned a target. The lead two troopers fired at the lead inside horse. The others aimed at the men on horseback prancing along the sides of the wagon.

The volley caught the robbers totally unprepared. The lead horse screamed as the slugs ripped into its head, and it stumbled and fell, snarling the harness and halting the slow-moving wagon. The two men on horseback both were downed, lying wounded on the ground beside the wagon.

Jim aimed coolly and fired again, bringing

down a man who had jumped from the wagon and run for a ditch. The rifles spoke again, and two more men tumbled from the wagon.

Steel wiped his hand over his face and looked through the darkness at Sergeant Foster.

"Let's go up and see what we have left."

Four of the six men were dead. The two others were so badly wounded they wouldn't live out the night. They were carried back to the ranch-house and laid on a patch of grass under the trees.

They cut the dead horse out of the harness, then turned the wagon around, and drove it back to the yard. The horses were unhitched and put in a small corral. That was when Jim remembered the old folks. He found a lantern, lit it, and went with Foster into the barn. The table and chairs were empty, and there was no sign of the couple.

They called and called, but could find no one. Wearily they searched the barn, probed into the hay, and when they still couldn't find the couple, Jim called loudly, explaining that the shooting was over, the bad men were all gone, and they could come out.

Nothing.

Jim and the men returned to the green grass under the trees, and stretched out for some sleep. A one-man guard was set up on a two-hour rotation, and then the troopers went to sleep.

Jim came awake instantly. He had heard something different. It was just dawn, and the light was coming stronger with every moment. The sounds came from the barn.

He was on his feet, running toward the barn with the guard, when the elderly man and woman came out, looked at Steel and waved, then passed right by him on their way to the ranchhouse.

A half hour later, Jim and Foster sat in the kitchen of the small ranchhouse, drank coffee and ate hash brown potatoes and fried eggs, drank milk and ate toast with crabapple jelly.

"Soon as I heard the shots, I knew we had trouble," the man said. "So Martha and me went into our hideout. This place has been here a long time. Used to be Indians around, and once or twice they scared us, so we built our Indian hideout. It's in the barn, but I won't tell you where. And it's underground, so we wouldn't get fried if them Indians burned down the barn out of spite.

"So last night Martha and me decided we better go under and wait it out. So, by crackey, we did."

Before they left, the soldiers buried the two ranch hands that had been killed, and, well down in a field, buried the robbers. The farmer had drawn up a map showing how they could make the trip back to Sacramento by road, which was shorter than the way they had come crosscountry. The roads weren't very good, but they would be easier and quicker. Sergeant Foster sent two men backtracking the first wagon, with instructions for the five troopers to take the wagon back to Sacramento.

Foster stood there thinking about the orders he had just given, and then he shook his head.

"Captain, I think I'll go with these two men. I don't want to put that kind of responsibility on them. I'll make sure all of these gold artifacts get back to the exhibit car, and we'll see you there." He saluted Jim, who gave him a snappy return salute as the other troopers watched in surprise.

They wished the farm couple a good summer, and said they would have the sheriff come by, then they headed out on the road. Jim took the reins of the wagon and drove it steadily, though slowly, back to Sacramento, with the other troopers following him.

Chapter Fourteen

Jim arrived back in Sacramento before Sergeant Foster and the other gold wagon had. As he pulled up in front of the exhibit car, he saw Margarita standing on the step, facing in.

"Hey, Margarita!" he yelled, getting down from the wagon.

"Jim!" she said, as she turned and saw him. Margarita ran down the steps and over to him.

"Is this all of the artifacts?" she said, looking at the wagon.

"No, just half," Jim said, watching as the soldiers who had ridden back with him dismounted, then stood guard on the gold in the wagon. "Sergeant Foster will be back with the rest soon. In fact, he should have been here by now."

"Oh, I hope that they did not run into trouble," she said. "Do you think they did?"

Jim laughed. "I doubt it," he said. "It was probably farther than the farmer thought it was."

"Farmer?" Margarita asked. "What farmer?"

Jim realized that she didn't know the story yet. "You'll know soon enough," he said. "I'm tired, and need a hot bath and a good meal."

"When will you tell me?" she asked.

"First, I have to take this horse back to the livery stable, and talk to the sheriff, and —"

"As director of this tour, I demand to know what happened." The words were harsh, but she said them gently, as if she felt she had to say them, though she didn't mean it.

Jim frowned, then shrugged. "First off, I have to do all these other things. Later, we'll see," he said, tipped his hat to Margarita, and walked over to the wagon, where the soldiers, saddle-weary but alert at their self-appointed posts, stood guarding the artifacts.

"If you men can hang in there for another few minutes, I'll round up some fresh guards. They've had enough rest."

The men thanked him, as Jim walked off toward the livery stable with his horse. He increased his speed sensing that Margarita was following him.

"Wait, Jim," she said, her voice breathy.

He stopped and turned to watch her walk toward him. When she got within five feet of the man, she stood still.

"I . . ." She hesitated. "I just wanted to thank you for recovering the artifacts. When I heard the story from that army man, I thought I'd never see them again. Oh! That reminds me. I must tell Señor Romero that they are back. I'm sure he'll want to inspect them with me."

"Only half of them are back," Jim corrected her, but as he said it, he heard a wagon approaching in the distance, and a few minutes later, the second load of gold relics rolled near the siding where the first stood.

Sergeant Foster, riding ahead on his horse, dismounted and smiled at Jim.

"Mission accomplished," he said, and then ordered his men to dismount and move the wagons together for safety.

"All of them are back now," Margarita said. "I'll hear the story from Sergeant Foster. I'm sure he won't be as busy as you seem to be."

Jim smiled and walked away to the livery stable, to turn in his horse. After that, he explained the situation to the sheriff, including the bodies they'd buried out there. An hour later, he headed to the hotel where he'd find the rest of his guards. They were eating, which was a surprise to Jim. It was nearly five o'clock! It had taken them longer than he had thought it would to get back to town from the farm.

He told the men to come to the car when they were through eating, and that all the gold had been recovered. Jim was hungry, but declined the meal offered to him. He was headed toward his hotel when he heard a voice calling him.

It was Romero, who stood near Margarita at the exhibit car. Jim walked to the two and greeted them.

"Mr. Steel, I don't know how to thank you for recovering all the artifacts. I must confess I never thought I'd see them again."

"It just takes a little work," Jim said. "But there's still a few things about this robbery that I'm not quite clear on," he said. "Think we can talk for a moment?"

Romero's face went pale. "Of course," he said.

Margarita walked over to sit with Tia Rosa on

a bench nearby that was shaded from the late afternoon sun, as Jim and Romero walked near the exhibit car.

Jim noticed that Romero was nervous, more so than he should have been. In fact, the man seemed to think that Jim was terribly upset with him.

"Alright," Jim said, after watching the man's nervousness. "Let's have it. What's bothering you?"

"Me?" Romero said, looking at Jim in shock. "I thought we were going to talk about the robbery."

"Maybe we are," Jim said, and stared hard at the man. Under his gaze, Romero finally looked down to the ground.

"Alright, alright," he said. "I can't hide it anymore."

"Can't hide what?" Jim asked.

"The robbery — it wasn't real. It was phony."

"What?" Jim said, staring at the man. He didn't believe him. "What are you talking about?"

"It wasn't real. Well, at least, not at first," Romero said, looking away from Jim's face.

"Are you trying to tell me that those ten men, two wagons of gold, and the rope that tied you to that tree weren't real? Are you feeling okay? Maybe you got a little too much sun."

"I — I wanted to do something that people would notice," Romero said. "I wanted to be the man of the moment, to get some attention, my name in the newspapers." He glanced over to

Margarita. "She's gotten most of it during the tour so far. Don't you think I deserve my share?" The man looked away, at the setting sun.

So that was it. The pieces fell together. Romero had faked the robbery, so that he could recover the gold and say he'd saved the day. The only trouble was that the men had found out what Romero was planning to do, and then wanted to keep the gold. So it had turned into a real robbery, and Romero really was tied up to that tree. Serves him right, Jim thought, for putting everyone through such hell for the last few days.

"What will become of me?" Romero asked.

"I don't know," Jim said.

"I'm just glad the artifacts are back and in perfect condition. It is a miracle that you were able to recover them all, and I am deeply in your debt."

"What about the eleven men who had to die for your chance to get your name in the newspaper?" Jim said bitterly. The man turned away from Jim. "Your name'll be in the newspapers. All over the front page of the *Sacramento Bee*!"

Margarita Contreras walked up at that moment and laid her hand on Jim's shoulder.

"Jim, I think you should reconsider. Yes, I heard everything, and I realize what Señor Romero has done. It is wrong, but the gold is safe, and I'm sure he won't do it again. Why do anything about it now?"

Jim smiled at the woman's sense of justice. "I won't do anything directly, other than contact the authorities. Señor Romero will have to get out of the United States and go back to Mexico soon. Whether the story about what happened will get out or not. . . ." Jim frowned. "It doesn't matter to me. Not now. You're right about that, Margarita. It's over."

She turned to look at Romero, but couldn't say anything. After a moment, she glanced at Jim, then walked to Tia Rosa, and together the women moved to their hotel as the sun set.

Jim had the urge to call after the women, but decided against it. He had time for dinner dates later. He still had Romero on his hands.

He took the man to the sheriff's office, and called in Barlow to help in the problem.

It was a sticky international incident, and no one was sure how to handle it, not even David John Barlow. But after several hours, they decided that Romero could spend the night in Sacramento, but he had to be on a train bound for Mexico in the morning. The official explanation for his resignation from the tour would be exhaustion, and that would have to satisfy everyone.

"In this manner," Barlow said, adjusting his glasses with his little finger, "this situation will be resolved, and no one will be hurt in the process. It would be an ugly mark on nearly all of our records," he said, glancing directly at Jim. "But no matter. It is finished, and no one need ever know the whole story."

Jim left the meeting and went back to the wagons, to make sure the men were working as planned. The glass panes had been removed from inside the train car, and Jim started the men loading the pieces back into the display case. He told them to put them down in any order, since Margarita would arrange them later.

He left Sergeant Foster in charge of the gold, telling him to set the guard when everything was reloaded in the car, and to lock the door. He gave the sergeant the exhibition car key, and said he was on his way to get a hot bath, a big dinner, and a long night's sleep.

Jim was through with the bath, and finishing his dinner in the dining room, when he thought again of the beautiful black-haired señorita, Margarita. He still had much work to do. He had to begin his campaign on Tia Rosa, to convince her that he could be trusted, and to gain her approval for a romantic dinner for two with Margarita . . . alone.

Then somewhere between here and Washington D.C., where the tour ended, he would again taste the sweetness of the lovely señorita's lips, and after that, it would be up to Margarita.

Jim smiled as he headed up to his room. At the end of the tour, he would have a thousand dollars in double-eagle gold coins, and would have made a friend or two. He smiled again thinking about the gold and Margarita. Right then, he wasn't sure he could choose between them if he had to. Instead, he would concentrate on having them both.

The employees of G.K. Hall hope you have enjoyed this Large Print book. All our Large Print titles are designed for easy reading, and all our books are made to last. Other G.K. Hall books are available at your library, through selected bookstores, or directly from us.

For information about titles, please call:

(800) 223-2336

To share your comments, please write:

Publisher
G.K. Hall & Co.
P.O. Box 159
Thorndike, ME 04986